Angelina T. Tyson

THE LOVE YOU DESERVE

AN EGOCENTRIC BILLIONAIRE LOVE STORY

SERIES ONE

TABLE OF CONTENT

Introduction

This book is a pure work of fiction. Names, events and everything isn't precisely based on real life.

Welcome to the journey of two soul bounded people who are worlds apart.

A romantic love story of a fatherless church girl, Isabella and an arrogant billionaire's son Carlos.

It all began when Isabella, a local vocalist in her church met Carlos a billionaire's son in a program he was invited to by his girl friend Antonia a popular philanthropist. Carlos developed likeness for Isabella which eventually turned into what we can call LOVE...continue reading to catch all the story as it unfolds from different Point of View (PoV).

Chapter One

Isabella's POV

I twisted down sliding my feet into my ugg sandal, shooting my eyes restlessly around to search for my handbag. A call got through, it's Camela, "Please accept my apologies I'll be there soon... yes I assured."

I'm late as damnation for the congregation program in which I'll be singing a performance. I'm not apprehensive, it's been something I've been doing for a really long time and I incredibly appreciate doing that not for the installment but rather the delight of singing gospel tunes to other brethren.

It gives outrageous joy into my heart serving and seeing individuals reflect on the expressions of the tune and magnify our Producer.

I surged out of my room which I share with my younger sibling into the parlor. My mother and Fabian sat on our nearly broken-down sofa. Mother was perusing her Book of scriptures while Fabian hunched behind the middle table getting her work done. "I'll see you all this evening, I love you."

"May God accompany you my dear." Mother kissed my cheeks and grinned at me, "I realize you'll do extraordinary as usual. I unsettled Fabian's hair carelessly and made rapidly for the entryway.

I'm fortunate my congregation is a twenty minutes stroll from my area and I would have no need to take a taxi and burn through cash, I can add to my reserve funds for my mom and Fabian's up keep.

My area isn't the best spot to grow up. It's underneath nice with obsolete structures scattered over the enormous land. Thrift shops line the roads and from time to time, irate taxi drivers yell at the individuals who have caused slow down on their tables which to have taken a larger part up to the street where vehicles should pass.

I shake my head and a bump structure in my throat. I breath in and out. I can't gamble with crying and wrecking my performance. In circumstances such as this I look on the more brilliant side to life. I'm working in a multi-million-dollar car organization as a secretary to the supervisor dissimilar to most young ladies in this village who either function as servers or strippers and I have all in all a sum in my investment funds. I'm expecting a raise soon so I can move my family out of this neighborhood to an all the more respectable one with a superior school for Fabian and a comfortable inclination for my mum who agonizes over the deficiency of my dad.

Ok that man, things were much simpler and life was a great deal agreeable than how it is currently when he was near. He filled in as a foreman for a consultancy firm for a really long time before his retirement. The person who assumed control over his office stole assets in my dad's name and he was faulted for it when the firm found out. They striped us of all the moderate abundance father obtained while working sincerely, leaving us with nothing, not so much as a penny.

The aggravation and distress from our quandary killed him, abandoning us with our mom who was likewise a resigned nearby teacher. Our poor monetary circumstance passed on her with a gentle stroke every once in a while, delivering her unequipped for attempting to fight for us. Hence, the obligation of cooking for our family fell upon me, being the oldest girl of the family.

I needed to sign up for a secretarial school to get a certificate that empowered me to earn the position I have. My fantasy about being a legal advisor is waiting currently, I'm attempting to set aside cash for that. It will require years yet I'm prepared to pause, my energy for it can't melt away soon.

I showed up at the congregation at 8:35pm and God being so great, it was my chance to perform. I think since I was late my name was opened for the last performer of the evening.

I can't be happier. Mr. Pedro the regular host for the greater part of our congregation programs declares to the assembly I'm the next and also the last performer for the evening.

"Go Isabella and favor the assemblage with your ministration!" My girlfriend Camela who's a Muslim shooed me away with an immense smile all over, pantomiming blowing kisses at me. The others around snickered at her activities. They were similarly invigorated for my ministration.

I went up stage and to be completely forthright I got somewhat anxious. The gathering has multiplied in size than our past programs. I breathe in and out, saying a quiet petition for God above to dominate and involve me as a vessel like he generally does. "Great evening fine people, I'm regarded to remain here to serve the gospel to you through a melody,

I'll ask you to think deeply about the words that are coming, for God to favor your life, so be it."

There was a high melody of so be it from the congregation. That warmed me up and shutting my eyes, I started:

"I was just a child, when I felt the Savior leading

I was drawn to what I could not understand

And for the cause of Christ, I have spent my days believing

That what He'd have me be, who I am

As I've come to see the weaker side of me

I realize His grace is what I'll need

When sin demanded justice for my soul

Mercy said no

I'm not going to let you go

I'm not going to let you slip away

You don't have to be afraid

Mercy said no

Sin will never take control

Life and death stood face to face

Darkness tried to steal my heart away

Thank You Jesus, Mercy said"

I realized, checking out at the congregation, actually singing. The majority of them were in tears, the words were so strong and the gathering was profoundly moved. A noisy cheer and round of acclaim emitted from the gathering as I sang the last line of the melody and bowed effortlessly. I appreciated God for the gift of live this evening.

Going behind the stage, Camela race to me, inundating me in a bone smashing embrace. Some of the time she neglects she's double the size of me and however we're both blended race, her skin was a hazier shade than mine and she was well proportioned than I'm. We both got a thick body, that we're saving for our future spouses as opposed to squandering it away in our childhood.

"Cammy, my ribs, let go off me you enormous teddy bear!" I squirmed out of her warm hug, slapping her hand, "what! have I warned you concerning your embraces?"

Camela scratched her neck, smiling timidly and stayed silent. Obviously, Cammy won't recall, regardless, she won't say it. Her embraces generally made me heave for air and my ribs hurt not that awful though for me to feel a slight aggravation. "I pardon you yet the present your last." Who? I'm I joking? I'll be telling her again very soon. Cammy...

"How about we go get some espresso." She proposed, taking my arm and hanging tight for reply. Espresso won't be bad at the moment and I'm longing for it too but the program isn't finished. I can't go else I'll get smashed by Mrs. Sara, my back up parent.

She's the bereft sister of the head minister, who helped my family and I when we initially moved here and assisted us with getting comfortable. Taking me under her consideration when I was just twelve years of age. I love her and dread her out and out. However, she's not terrifying. Mrs. Sara is the most mindful and friendly individual I've at any point met yet when you screw with her, you're disciplined. She will endlessly address you and when she's done scoop you in her arms and punish your hand. Indeed, that is the way she is. "The program isn't finished at this point; you don't want to get on Mrs. Sara's awful side, isn't it, right?"

I saw a change in her countenance. She's recalling her most recent discipline from getting on her terrible side. Cammy needed to scour the entire church and clean wherever subsequently and do you know her wrongdoing? She neglected to switch off the tap in the women washroom on Sunday and on Monday, there was insight about the women washroom overwhelmed and after Mrs. Sara questioned us, Cammy admitted to it saying it was a mix-up.

She didn't pull it off. Nobody pulls off a wrongdoing with Mrs. Sara around. However, she's severe, we as a whole love and revere her, admiring her as a protective figure in our disturbing times. "It will be over in 5,4,3,2 and 1!" Cammy did the commencement, peering down at her wristwatch, "we can go get that velvety espresso with no obstruction."

"Insane Cammy!" I dragged her from where we sat and adjusted my bag appropriately on my shoulder. We walked connected at the hip to our number one cafe and picked our standard table in the corner sitting above the vehicle leave.

The coffee shop radiates a comfortable inclination and a tranquil climate. However, it's not exactly costly, it's the brilliant shop in this piece of our destitution ridden area, serving heavenly baked goods and delectable espressos I'm yet to taste elsewhere. Jorge, our record-breaking server waltz towards us, smiling from one ear to another. I know why, moving my eyes to Cammy, I tracked down her cheeks a brilliant shade of red. I smell love all around. These two are one befuddled pair I've at any point met in my life, they're so obsessed with one another one day and the following they can't stand one another.

"The standard thing?" He asked us, taking out his notebook and looking at Cammy with a look I can't understand.

"Indeed, and negative, I need mocha to the surprise of no one except for I'll match it with a lemon ginger blueberry biscuit." I've been seeing it on their menu yet never requested, today I need to have a vibe of how it's like and perhaps request it every once in a while, assuming I ought to get exhausted of my typical doughnut with vanilla frosting. Cammy gazed at me with protruding eyes. It's been years I met Cammy and whenever we come here, it's dependably doughnut I request so I get why she's like this. She had a go at persuading me so often to attempt different stuffs like her number1 chocolate plunged sesame treats. I won't ever yield. "Definitely, Yep, no doubt. I change whenever I need; you can allude to me as a chameleon definitely." I spun a strand of my obstinate fixed hair that actually looks afro around my finger and winked at her.

"OK miss chameleon and to you, I need my usual because a few of us still need to be human." She chuckled at her words so did Jorge. No big surprise both of you are a couple.

"I'll be back instantly ladies."

"Alright." We said sat discussing arbitrary topics. The local now, our present positions, cooking shows and where we see ourselves in years to come.

Chapter Two

Carlos's POV

"May we at any point get moving?" I eagerly request my pal from numerous years, Antonia Manuel Juan. Your regular style goddess. She welcomed me to a melodic program at her congregation, Realm Baptist and here she is deferring us with reapplying her make up.

At times I can't help thinking about how I finished being dearest companions with her, she's flighty. I continued to think about how a style goddess like her is going for a congregation program on a Friday night. Don't misunderstand me however we as a whole realize these goddesses favor going to mold shows and busying themselves with most stylish trend patterns than being somewhere else.

Brief she's in Italy, doing a demonstrating gig, the following she's in Dubai traveling endlessly and the following she's in Africa assisting battle with drafting regions with cash. She has a major heart and I realize that attracted me to her.

Antonia actually looks at her face once again in the mirror and went to me batting her long lashes at me, "how do I look boo?"

"You know by now and I will keep telling you; now and always, it's no joke." She's always wearing the look - pretty - come what may. Her model like body valuing any dress tossed her direction. It's a secret to our loved ones why we aren't together after so long. The response is straightforward, I think of her as a sister. I'm not strict yet I'm certainly not submitting that evil entity with somebody I consider to be a blood.

She feigned exacerbation and sulked, "don't I look faultless? Don't I speak to you?" "Move past yourself love, we're now late. "I told her giggling and escaped the vehicle. Antonia hammered the entryway in fierceness and followed off without me.

I love her without a doubt however when it gets to circumstances such as these, I need to choke her. Lmao simply joking yet she effectively lashes out over little and immaterial issues.

I shook my head and entered the congregation. The congregation was completely stuffed for a Friday night. I filtered the region searching for where Antonia is situated. I in the long run found her sitting alone on a seat four seats from me. Approaching her, I plunked down and took out my telephone to message my different companions. They arranged a Friday night out at the club. My endorsement to accompany Antonia here was offhand so I must text them to do without me.

"So next on our rundown is the last performer for the evening, with a series of commendation, how about we invite our own special singing star, Isabella." The host said with fervor into the mouthpiece. The group cheered at the alleged Isabella. She is by all accounts renowned and a number1 around here. "Who's Isabella?" My inquiry wasn't responded to when the lady being referred to came up in front of an audience., she looks sort of natural, it resembles I know her from some place yet can't recollect where. There was nothing unprecedented about her, she was wearing a basic African print dress. Her normal hair in a major bun on her head and feet shrouded in a slipper I feigned exacerbation, such a lot of quarrel and energy over nothing.

I was even exhausted and took out my telephone to check my Instagram account where I order a gigantic fan base. There were a couple of post from my friend Luis carrying on with their best life.

Isabella or anything that her name is made a sound as if to speak and grinned. I heaved in irritation, hustle the hellfire along and we should get outta here.

"Great evening fine people, I'm respected to remain here to serve the gospel to you through a melody,

I'll ask you to ponder the words that are coming, for God to favor your life, so be it." Did she come to give a discourse or a goddamn tune?

"I was just a child, when I felt the Savior leading

I was drawn to what I could not understand

And for the cause of Christ, I have spent my days believing

That what He'd have me be, who I am

As I've come to see the weaker side of me

I realize His grace is what I'll need

When sin demanded justice for my soul

Mercy said no

I'm not going to let you go

I'm not going to let you slip away

You don't have to be afraid

Mercy said no

Sin will never take control

Life and death stood face to face

Darkness tried to steal my heart away

Thank You Jesus, Mercy said"

I opened my mouth wide, staggered. My demeanor reflected those around. My skin was shrouded in goosebumps, there are conceived artists and prepared vocalists. This lady remaining in front of an audience right presently is a conceived vocalist, she's the young lady with the large voice. She's that somewhat young lady who's singing floods your skin with goosebumps, yes, she's that.

She completed her performance and bowed nimbly. "Yet again thank you." With that she gave back the mic to the host and left the stage.

"Who's she?" I thought of how to ask Antonia who is now quiet and cold.

"She's the lead vocalist and singing star here, not much." She shrugged her shoulders and returned to composing on her telephone. I can't help thinking about what she came here for. The main thing she's being doing since we showed up is type furiously on her telephone, heaving once in a while.

"Something really stands out about her, simply pay attention to her voice." I preclude every one of the negative things I said about her before. This young lady is exceptional, I'm somewhat stricken by her however no chance is she, my class. I lean toward my young lady's hot and tasteful, they're a decent hotshot during grants and occasions. She's excessively basic and easygoing to have a possibility of being with me.

I daydreamed the remainder of the talking being made and focused on my telephone. I'm anticipating handling a date with this new model I'm attempting to attach with for the interim. I don't do connections, indulgences and friends with benefits somewhat thing.

They're much simpler than connections, there's no getting sentiments in this. I felt somebody pull at my hand. I raised my head to see Antonia with an exhausted look, "the program is finished, how about we go."

"I don't have the foggiest idea what we came here for."

"I was welcome, that is the reason."

"Furthermore, you decided to drag me here with you as well?"

"What are friends for."

"Hello I think I know you." A young lady came dependent upon us, grinning comprehensively. The lady next to her, similarly gave an expansive grin. "It's Carlos Santiago, my number one performer ever." She screeched uproariously causing the others around to check us out. They additionally panted and advancing toward us.

Gracious gosh, not this evening. Antonia acted the hero, "sorry folks this evening is a terrible time, we vow to return again only for a meet and welcome. Until further notice, I would need to take him away." She streaked them a phony grin and held my hand prepared to drag me away.

"I can recall you as well, you're now and again in disguise and sit at the back when you come to church however, I know it's you, trendsetter Antonia Manuel Juan." A youngster shouted rising with fervor.

"A reminder, we will come back for a hang out." She dragged me out from the group. We strolled energetically to the vehicle and got in. I inhaled out feeling better, "golly that was close, I was in no temperament to meet with my fans."

"You forever aren't in the temperament." She ignites the vehicle and hurried away. I found individuals pointing at the vehicle with looks favorably upon their appearances. They're most likely telling their friends they saw us. I like gathering with my fans however now and again it gets so tiring. I somewhat hate it off late most particularly when I've had some time off from my profession to zero in additional on our family auto domain and I'll be beginning work on Monday.

Discussing that, wow, I have a meeting for certain clients tomorrow, which is my first undertaking appointed to me by my dad and assuming the gathering goes as arranged boo hoo, we're moving from very rich people to multi billionaires. Goodness yes! What's more, conceivably make me the likely successor to the realm out of my three kin and learn to expect the unexpected. Most extravagant entertainer on the planet, how can it sound? Phenomenal! Yep, no doubt.

Chapter Three

Carlos's POV

Today is the day, I at last resume work at my dad's vehicle organization not as the honor winning entertainer I am but rather as the child and new worker of the organization, Santiago car enterprise.

I'm not really eager to be beginning work today. To me the corporate world is exhausting and lifeless and fun. Acting drives everything and everyone, the following up on set, film debuting and the honor shows all makes the acting scene energetic and a ceaseless wellspring of fun.

The porter of the organization opened the entryway and offered his appreciation welcoming me, "Great morning, Sir."

"Good morning Scratch Kringle." I answered him in a droning voice.

"Welcome and have a pleasant day." He offered his appreciation once again, smiling at me like a bonehead. I gestured, venturing into the organization's office entrance hall. Commotion, developments and everything stopped. Everyone's eyes were stuck on me, taking in everything I might do and step. The spot was so tranquil, I want to hear the pulsating of their souls and how it's so quick.

This is the response I get whenever I come here. The women play with me every which way to stand out enough to be noticed. I barely give them one, today like generally I cover my face with a scary look, scarcely looking at them and advanced toward the lift.

Our family's private lift, we share with no staff regardless of how unique you are. My family is your standard bombastic and egotistical well off classed individuals who give no hoot to the people who end up winding up in the lower class of the social ladder. That was the manner by which I was brought up. The characteristic is in me however a large portion of my partner entertainer's whine. I was sustained to be that, it's not really my issue. Old propensities stalwart, as they say.

I ventured into my office passing by the work area of my recently utilized individual associate. She rose from her seat and loosened up her hand, batting her lashes and giving me those enchanting eyes, scandalous women know best. "Good morning sir." She murmured and however today is whenever I first have focused on her, her voice resembles a nonsense talk in my ears. So pointless and irritating. I intellectually feigned exacerbation, fighting the temptation to fire her. It's my first day and hers also. I plan of working with her to check whether she's fit for working like she's equipped for tempting her supervisor on his first day of work. Shame to female species! "Present to me my timetable for today."

"OK sir, I'll be there in a jiffy."

"Be here the moment I step my legs into my office or you're terminated!" I smirked and loosed my tie a bit. Her presence and voice are choking me and has of nowhere made my tie tighter than I made it at home.

I don't have the foggiest idea how she figured out how to take out my timetable in a rush. She created it to me the moment I ventured into my office. "Read them out so anyone can hear." I said heading toward my work area. Dashing my eyes around, I took in the presence of my office.

It's simply the manner in which I love it. High contrast dividers with Valeria furnishings. It shows it's a manly office for an advanced and exemplary man like me. I plunked down behind my work area, crossing legs and investigated my watch, "the clock is ticking miss...?"

"Miss Valeria." Miss Valeria pushed her chest out, once more, brushing her hair with her fingers and batted her lashes. I was enticed to inquire as to whether she has an eye issue however halted myself and took a gander at her in irritation.

She's truly driving me crazy. "This is an office and not a sensation exhibition, read the damn paper in your hand and stop this uncertain putrid teaser. I don't do young ladies like you." I said tranquilly, my words going against my tone.

She quit batting her lashes and her enticing eyes, busted with outrage. I giggled inside me, who in the world does she believe she's blowing up at? Me? Young lady gimme a break I care less. You don't take care of me or add more cash to my wealth.

"Sorry sir." She gulped hard saying 'sorry'

"Begin!" By this time, my understanding was a twine workshop as I get to work trying to add impact to every word I uttered.

"You eat at 7:30, arranging with the organization's staff at 10, meeting with your dad a short time later, you eat at your number1 eatery and a comprehensive gathering with the loading up of managers of the organization till 4 in the evening."

I shot her an incredulous take care of going over what she just said in my mind. A few words didn't sound right to my ears. "Did you say I have what with the organization's staffs at 10?"

"Arranging sir."

"Who employed you?" I requested from her, whirling the ball point pen in the middle of my fingers. I raised my head to meet her look currently on me. Who sane recruit a colleague as stupid as this who clearly disapproves of her vocabulary.

"The Human Resourcing Supervisor Sir." Simply check that out!

"Did you rest as you would prefer through?"

"No sir."

She shook her head suddenly and augment her eyes in shock at my inquiry. Her eyes streaked with outrage once more. I was additionally furious with her answer, it didn't appear to be certified however I didn't test further. I knew what I had as a main priority.

"Leave my office, I'll hit you up." I told her with a pompous rush of my left hand which I got the telephone collector with.

I'm calling that director at the present time and let him know some appropriately harsh criticism. He's so going to lose his employment; this isn't the initial time he's utilized women as idiotic as her. He gives them work in return for between the legs favors.

"Serve me some hot espresso, Valeria with no sugar and milk."

"OK sir." She rushed quickly out of my office swinging her hips, not at all annoyed by her idiocy.

Chapter Four

Carlos's POV

"Carlos work with her for the interim. I'll actually ensure, you get another colleague." My dad said for the millionth opportunity since I came into his office. I can't understand the reason why he's so unyielding on changing that numb nut of an associate I have next to me of the organization.

I've been tenderly persuading him to adjust his perspective and it has yielded nothing. It's no time like the present I play the most difficult way possible, "fine father, in the event that you won't change her now. Think of me as a surrendered worker till you get me another collaborator."

I sneered at him, calculating my head to look at him straight without flinching. It's possibly he changes her now or I go by my promise. My dad needs me more than I need to associate with this organization. He will doubtlessly not deny me, I've bedeviled him in a way he can't get out. A commendation for the most brilliant ass!

"Fine, I'll get you another one before the day's over." He heaved in inconvenience and in shame, squeezing the scaffold of his nose.

"Better late than never, I'll meet you at the meeting room in a short time." I stood up from my seat with a quality of certainty. I'm a vital character here. Father says my prosperity and magnificence in the amusement world is really great for business. Nearly everybody would need to work with the most youthful and best entertainer bursting at the seams with the great searches for exposure and marking and minds for more imaginative undertakings. That is the fundamental justification for why I'm here, to utilize them to send our organization to the best heights.

My father truly cherishes cash. It's not his issue, he was brought into the world with a silver spoon and at a youthful age was given the obligation of running this organization till it became who it is today, a top brand and an easily recognized name here and the world round.

I'm anticipating taking more time to more noteworthy statures and for that to occur, I want a difference in private colleague and a breathing space away from these modest whorish ladies at the organization. I know every one of them, they're no different either way. Being a tease until you take more time to bed and begin falling in love and thereafter, worm their direction into appreciating abundance they didn't perspire for.

That is one motivation behind why I don't do connections. I do excursions and friends with benefits somewhat, I think. They're way more straightforward than connections and there's no falling in love.

Isabella's POV

Today there were quieted murmurs around the workplace, the haughty child of our manager has begun work at the organization. A considerable lot of the women here during breakfast and lunch we spouting over him. Respecting him for the most part for his notoriety as an honor winning entertainer for a long time and his god like build.

I heard a gathering of ladies who were close to my table discussing him.

"God! Truly I'll be his digger just to get a piece of that body." I was exceptionally frustrated at her feeble and modest reasoning. How can you energetically decide to be a digger for a pompous charlatan like him? Wow a few ladies need inoculations of normal sense.

Her companion wasn't any better. "I'm thinking of going to the Gucci store at the city center to get a few hot straps and also go get enticing cloths after work. I'll wear them tomorrow and go to his office with the reason I've been shipped off him and allure him. No man turns down a body like this." She ran her fingers on her body, licking her lips.

I heaved in my seat, truly? Good gracious women currently are so modest. The body she's so glad for, young lady certain individuals like us have it all the more yet don't involve it for evil delights in our old maid days.

I needed to wrap up my food rapidly and escape our cafeteria. The despicable remarks and murmurs around me made me need to choke and a while later let them know some appropriately harsh criticism. My partner and just friend at work, Sebastian, giggled at me the whole time. Letting me know I would before long be saying stuffs like that once I set my eyes upon him. I've met him and I know his face, better believe it he's fine and everything except that doesn't mean, I ought to make a special effort in luring him and inspire him to lay down with me for what? A few minutes or long stretches of joy that leaves culpability and disgrace subsequently? Not this time, I'm way better compared to that.

"I'll see you after work erh." I headed out in different directions from Jayson, strolling energetically to my work area. My manager has a meeting with different sheets of bosses in a short time to acquaint his child with them as a worker formally. He expected me to be there and take notes.

The way to my supervisor's office squeaks open, uncovering Satan himself. He passed by without saying a word and left with his mischievous advances. I didn't miss.

Truly, I don't think I'll be comfortable working under somebody as arrogant as him. His gazes debase you further in his eyes and from what I've known about him, he's most certainly going to be a grouchy and fussy boss.

His dad isn't the most pleasant boss yet he's not terrible by the same token.

He's very much like his child yet in a more restrained manner. I fished my standard meeting scratch pad out of my cabinet and took a pen. Setting it conveniently in the center of the cushion, I take swings from my filtered water and strolled off to the meeting room.

Yet again I met, Satan himself at the entry. He didn't take a gander at with disdain like previously, essentially passing by without a word. Why am I not amazed? It's so similar to him. He made the way for the room and banged it in my face. Had I not made a stride back, I'll be on my way right now to the organization's hospital with an enlarged temple.

Sitting down right adjacent to my boss, I looked around, ticking participation of the people who were available and when I was done shut my book and plunked down discreetly trusting that the meeting will start.

My supervisor stood up, making a sound as if to speak. He filtered the managers and when he was fulfilled, opened his mouth, tending to them. "I invite you all to this gathering. I'm mindful there shouldn't be an executive gathering during the current month. Something came up which all of you know, my child here," he motioned to his child who stayed there with a boring look, "he has joined the organization and beginning from today, he's taking the place of the CEO of this organization. Before you get clarification on some pressing issues, I need to make you mindful, I'll in any case be dynamic yet all of you need to manage him in all matters."

"Is it true that he is ready and mindful of the work before on him now? This isn't a tryout or a film scene. I want to find out whether he realizes what's involve in a corporate world." Mr. Diego Allan asked with scorn composed all around his face. "Indeed, he's particularly mindful of his obligations, that is the reason I said I'll in any case be dynamic. Assuming he has a trouble, he can come to me whenever and I'll help."

One more man put before the managers his view regarding this situation. Numerous others participated; I took a look at Satan himself. He sat in his seat, tapping his fingers on the table, unperturbed a piece at the conversation about him going round the table.

I deflected my eyes, peering down on my paper to forestall being caught. I haven't composed a lot of other than the participation and a few important focuses, three men set forward. The gathering was at last done and dusted. I inhaled out feeling much better, it got exhausting when it was approaching the end.

Greater part of the board individuals are not excited about their concept of villain himself accepting the situation as the President. My manager needed to bore into their skulls, the way that he possesses the organization and larger part of the offers in it. Qualifying him to do what we he feels right and needs be done. The managers shut up. Their portions in the organization can be effortlessly purchased by the offspring of my Mr. Santiago, my President. I have barely any insight into them however I've heard they're exceptionally rich. A normal model is our most up to date President here who thinks his cash and him matters more than others. Such individuals make me debilitated; they make me need hurl all my food all over and a short time later advise them to proceed to suffocate themselves in the Pacific Sea.

Assuming that I at any point become hopelessly enamored God, satisfy not one of these grandiose well-off individuals. I can't say I disdain them Ruler however to be completely forthright with you Father, I could do without them much. I murmured and assembled my things before I left, Mr. Santiago's voice requested me to get the rest free from his timetable. What a surprisingly good development, I can have the remainder of the day to myself and learn on the organization's PC. Yippeeeee!

Chapter Five

Whoever parties on work day they have work on the following day? It's no one else than me and only me. I'm having the bitchiest of headaches right, not good enough for a Tuesday morning subsequent to being presented as the new President of this organization. Yet, hello what difference does it make? I'm the chief and I do anything I desire, dislike I love this work in any case. I'm doing it for my dad and the family organization. Also, if not for that, I'll backtrack my means back to my vehicle without so much as a second thought to check the structure out.

A priggish grin observes it way to my lips as I cleaned my base lip with my thumb when I recollected what went down the earlier evening. I went through my night yesterday out at a lavish club with the model I've been attempting to attach with for at some point now. She was anything but a difficult one to figure out however she was putting on a show. One kiss on those stout lips and she was at my feet asking for additional, twerking on me and giving me a psyche blowing lap dance I had never had. She let me know she used to be a stripper and that was the most ideal justification behind her great dance moves.

The club was claimed by my companion and he had his servers serve us with heaps of costly tequilas, glasses of margaritas and martinis. I wasn't quite as squandered as Sofia who kept striping at the hidden part of the club requesting a fast in and out. She looked so frantic in those days in any event, when I squandered off her advances and solicitation. What's more, I was like truly? I love my young ladies level-headed, not smelling of liquor. It will make me gag and vomit on anything.

After we left the club and returned home to mine, I needed to mind over the course of the night till she nodded off. I'm no sitter except for I got it done, in the event that in her smashed state she ruins nostalgic things in my house.

I was unable to get any rest during the evening or toward the beginning of the day either, Sofia allured me into laying down with her when she awakened to demonstrate of her gratitude for bringing her home and keeping an eye on.

Why should I reject? I'm a full bloodied man all things considered; sex is something I can't reject like here we go. We continued forever till I was exhausted and somewhat numb however wasn't so powerless to come to work. I dislike it but rather it's for the family, family starts things out in all angles, regardless of what.

"Meet me here after work." I told my driver however it seemed like a request. He gestured, coming towards my side of the vehicle and opened the entryway. I got out of it and placed on my shades, the sun wasn't yet out yet I needed to and what I need is my specialty.

I got similar response from the representatives, the meeting fell quiet and like generally I took a gander at the drearily. Expanding my steps, I left the gathering into the lift and busied myself by perusing my telephone.

I got a couple of female workers gape at me on my way and trust me, it was aggravating. "Return to your work areas!" I asked for them with an indifferent expression.

I passed by the work area of my new collaborator subsequent to escaping the lift and strolling towards my office. I felt outrage preparing within when I investigated at their work area and figured out there was not a single damn soul to be found.

Was my dad pooping me? Or on the other hand is that my new associate isn't reliable. In the event that it's the last option, o kid she or he is in for a ride of their lives with me. I will ensure they quit on the off chance that they don't fulfill my guidelines. They've substantiated themselves they are not remotely close to my guidelines.

Right off the bat by not being here on time when I the supervisor who might have picked, is as of now here. I went into my office shaking my head.

There weren't no documents at all around my work area hanging tight for me, no espresso as a matter of fact no nothing. "What a futile reason of an individual do I have for an individual aide?" I asked myself in unbelief prior to bowing my hand. I brushed the hand of the suit coat upwards a bit and really look at the time on my watch.

It's 8:40am, I found out and work ought to have initiated an hour prior and I'm stuck here doing literally nothing. All in light of the fact that my futile reason of an aide is mysteriously gone. Most likely, she hasn't answered to work yet.

"If!" I verbally processed and run my hands through my coal black wavy hair which is getting neck length and eliminated my shades. It was no falsehood that I was nowhere near cheerful about this. How would I demonstrate my proficiency and making the organization thrive sitting idle? Not so much as some espresso to sooth my annoyance and these goddamn specialists will hope to be paid toward the month's end! Is it true or not that they are squandering our cash? Cash that can be utilized for other beneficial business. A delicate thump on my entryway made me turn my head strongly towards it and prepared to deliver my indignation on whoever strolls in. The Valeria woman who's my dad's very own associate strolled in, holding documents close by and a demeanor of certainty, I so gravely need to squash. I don't have any idea why yet I simply need to, perhaps in light of the fact that I'm furious and in light of the fact that she was a laborer here. My resentment wasn't just aimed at my uncouth colleague, it was aimed at every one of the workers of our organization.

"Good morning sir." She obligingly welcomed not saving me a grin like the women do around here. That was strangely new, such things don't occur to me around here. "Keep your great morning, what the heck do you need?" I requested smoothly in spite of myself. She kept up with her stance, obviously unflinching by my inconsiderateness. "I'm your new right-hand sir, I got-"

I didn't permit her pour out the remainder of the discourse or acquaintance or anything she desires with call it. I cut her off, it was at that point to the point of opening words. I didn't require her to squander her energy proclaiming the words, it wasn't like I gave it a second thought, in any case. She was simply going to put it to use for how I'm going to treat her.

"Who made you? I never mentioned for somebody like you. Whorish women, alluring their supervisors, I'm finished with women so return the same way you came and tell whoever sent you that I Don't Need a Prostitute! "Now my consideration is insignificant, not only is she my new woman right hand yet additionally had the audacity to resume work late, waking in with majestically and presenting herself.

Yet again she amazed me. No, I wouldn't agree astounded, she infuriated me more by not wincing at my sharp tone or my selections of words, I depicted her with when I was tending to her.

"I am sorry however your dad gave me plain orders to be your temporary individual aide till the one left has been replaced, sir." She told me with an indifferent presence however her final word resembled an insult. This young lady actually has balls remaining there, looking at me without flinching with that certainty emanating around her.

I see she's truly ready to work under me. Extraordinary, I fastened my hands together and laid them around my work area. We will check whether she can keep up with this quiet stance and walk certainly into my office beginning from now. I thought in my mind and grinned skeptically.

I'll ensure she stops working for me without me terminating me. I grinned again at myself, so happy with my groundbreaking thought, "get me my number one espresso in a moment."

"These are the documents you'll require for the afternoon" she gave me the records. I deliberately brushed my fingers against hers to confuse her as I took the documents, it will provide me with the fulfillment of seeing her awkward and her certainty breaking a bit. Or on the other hand standby would she say she is very much like the women around here? Cultivators, perhaps she will cherish it and show her genuine nature. "What's your number1 sir."

I glinted my eyes to her and checked out at her in stunningness and disarray. It's either this woman has an incredible capacity to conceal her feelings or she isn't annoyed when somebody plays with her, which that wouldn't shock me in the least. After the entirety of she's a specialist here and is very much like the others.

She asked from me with a similar face and tone she's been utilizing since she arrived. "Tell me the truth, my dad gave you plain orders to be my temp aide, yes or no? I'm certain he has informed you on my preferences so go! " I supposed and demanded with arrogance waiting in my voice as I acquired her words, she uttered at least two minutes before.

I recognized a little aversion easily as she pivoted to leave. I grinned, glad that I've at long last gotten a response from her which isn't remotely close to certainty and regardless of whether it was only a tad.

She's so mixed up assuming she thinks I'll make her visit here awesome. Be ready to stop my dear assistant.... standby I don't have the foggiest idea about her name. Who doesn't acquaint themselves with their boss?

Botch number three. The first is late and the second is she's Aurelia so certain, as opposed to what I need from her, I ought to be the sure one here since I rule! Her third mix-up isn't acquainting herself with me. I realize I didn't allow her an opportunity to. I couldn't care less, dislike I'm keen on her name, anyway.

I understood she looks recognizable like somebody I've met outside of here who somewhat won my love. Nah she can't be my Isabella, she's no chance like her. Huh did I simply say my? Gracious gosh what's up with me? Calling her mine however she isn't, I'll ensure she is yet for the time being allowed me to manage this supposed colleague of mine.

I took the documents she gave me that I had disposed of around my work area and spread them on the table. I was trying to looking through the second document when Miss sure returned, grasping a plate with espresso on. She put it on the table and pushed it before me. "Your espresso sir."

I gazed at the espresso on my table, thinking about how to irritate her. I thought hard till I had a thought. I took the cup, taking a taste of the substance and spat it on my table. I raised my head to take a gander at her decisively in the face, she has aggravated me more.

Indeed, this woman here has committed an error. She's gotten my number one espresso right, the fixings in their right extent. Simply the manner in which I love it however heartbroken. "Who in god's name prepared this espresso and told you my preferred?" I yelled at her, cleaning my mouth however I like the flavor of the espresso. I can't ruin my disguise by licking my lips.

"Sir, I thought most men like their espresso Valeria with no sugar and solid." I saw she wrinkled her temples in disarray as she expressed that, excusing my tone.

She lifted her hand and laid it on her hips before she breathed out intensely and strolled to the edge of my office. I took a gander at her this while and looked as she opened one bureau and drew out a tissue box from it.

She strolled nearer to the work area and cleared the table wipe in the wake of removing out tissues from it. She didn't care about my salivation was saved in the espresso when I spilled it out.

I gazed at her and pondered, why this young lady continues to be correct and a holy person? I've yelled at her and been inconsiderate to her yet she's unperturbed, going about her responsibilities like she minds less. "I'm not most men, I'm Carlos Santiago. Your chief and best entertainer within recent memory." I expressed priggishly after she was done and escaping my seat, I pointed my finger at her like I was cautioning her. "Tune in here miss anything your name is, go get me my number1 espresso. I don't mind the times you go out to get me, everything I really do think often about is you getting me my favorite!"

She looked pass my sharp finger. "I am Isabella Valentina Romeo, sir." Her name carried out of her lips impeccably and when she was done, she tightened her lips.

"I don't care what your name is, just go get me my espresso the way I like is prepared!" I hollered at her and stopped when I understood the clench hand name she said. Stand by, did she simply say she's Isabella? Like the young lady who has me stricken? It can't be, that young lady was so streamlined. My associate is as well yet they're so divergent in their looks yet comparable with their facial look.

Taking a gander at my collaborator, she previously had her eyes on me. She remained there persistently and not uttering a word. I felt she thought I had one more assignment for her. I didn't and excused her with the rush of my hand.

Isabella. I recalled her name from when Antonia let me know when I asked her and let out a timid grin subsequent to plunking down. I followed my fingers all the rage and started to contemplate her. That lovely woman has gotten me stricken without knowing. Her huge resonant sweet voice that overflowed me with goosebumps is as yet ringing in my ears. However, i need to search for her, I've been pondering her since I met her. I simply don't have the foggiest idea what's going on with me. It's not normal for me to get interested by a tasteful and hot. woman. A woman who doesn't have cash joined to her name, I've been told since I was a girl, young ladies like that are go getters and my couple of experiences with ladies in that class in the past have validated it.

Chapter Six

Isabella's POV

Destiny related to my supervisor chose to play with me today. I was so blissful in the first part of the day, awakening to a humorous joke from Sebastian and my mom beating previously. She can now move her right hand with no assistance and may before long be up on her feet like previously. Nothing will give me such a lot of delight than seeing her returning to her old self, so brimming with life and trust.

She's continuously going to me my good example for staying with my dad through various challenges and putting forth a valiant effort to bring us up in a manner most guardians are jealous of. I was at my work area, transmitting satisfaction in my work when Mr. Santiago strolled in. He requested that I pack my stuffs out of my office. I was befuddled and devastated at first, thinking I was being sacked thinking about the progressions in the organization yesterday.

I was feeling better when he said he wasn't terminating me yet taking more time to another office and think about who my supervisor is individuals; Satan himself.

Argh you can envision my disappointment then, at that point, being approached to work under him. I will favor being sacked to working for him. He doesn't respect me and just ganders at me with disdain, days he sees I exist in his reality.

How might I function for him? What ensures his demeanor will change and most particularly what ensures I'll most recent a moment with him. Moan this is the time I need to practice all the tolerance I've been shown such a long time.

I was late to my new office and truly, I couldn't have cared less. It wasn't my shortcoming; I didn't realize I'll leave my place of refuge for Satan's sanctuary today. I previously had the records he will require for the afternoon so I went into his office to hand them over to him, keeping an expert face and mysteriously procured a demeanor of certainty I didn't realize I had.

Knowing him, however little, he will successfully irritate me. I went ready to his office to forget about any impolite remark or conduct towards me and work like nobody's business till the day is finished.

Envision the quality of pomposity and disposition he tossed at me. Requesting that I escape his office and calling me a skank. I didn't expect less from him, his looks says everything. I couldn't say whether he generally disapproves of an unfortunate woman that has made him so unpleasant and who he is towards ladies of our group.

He then advised me to get him his number one espresso taking the records from me and brushing his fingers against mine and afterward taking a gander at my face to see a response, I stayed impartial. I won't provide him with the fulfillment of getting a response from me. Satan himself didn't let me know his number one espresso. How on earth does he anticipate that I should be aware? since I can't ask his dad and he won't tell me all things   considered.

I got him a hot cup of Valeria espresso with no sugar, simply the manner in which most men like it, Valeria and solid. He spat the espresso on his table, yelling at me who made the espresso and let me know it's his number1. I needed to clean his stained table, actually practicing all the persistence I have, not to explode and let him know some appropriately harsh criticism. That is most likely going to get me terminated however I couldn't care less. I'm poor however I'm human, I merit regard!

He requested me to get him his number1 espresso and doesn't mind the number of times I go, all he really wants is his damn espresso. I went all through his office to the bistro neighboring the structure on in excess of five events till he chose a mug of coffee, letting me know it's not his number1 however he'll consider on the grounds that he believes me should address a task for him.

The task was me to go to the shopping center far away from the organization to get him a crate of chocolate and a jug of wine. I did as such, protesting faintly, taking a taxi with my own cash after he would not give me an admission. That demon, does he suppose I have cash in excess and toss around as he does?

I finished my task, returning to the workplace. He was in there with a wonderful slim lady who evaluated me, giving me a quiet envious mentality. I intellectually feigned exacerbation, does she suppose I care about him? Not to mention adore him affectionately? Smh.

He took the gifts from me and waved his hand excusing me, returning to sucking faces with the woman on his laps. Ewww who likes watching their supervisor do that before them. I needed to choke and show them how nauseating they're looking doing that.

I left going to my office and plunked down to advance for a spell on the PC around my work area. I was so immersed in learning criminal regulation, I didn't hear him come in, accompanying the woman out. He stepped relaxed into my office and took out something from his front pocket, "arrange off this." He tossed them on my table.

Ewwwwwwww! It was a radiant red net strap that he tossed on it. He glinted his eyes to me with a self-satisfied grin and followed off egotistically. Argh! Who does he suppose he is? Since I work for him doesn't mean he can inspire me to do any nauseating thing.

I didn't get to see what they did yet he having her strap in his pocket lets me know it was awful and nauseating. I'm never entering his office till that spot is purified with blessed water and cleaned a short time later. I can envision the negative air there the present moment.

Eww, the strap needs to get off my work area to permit me have a breathing and working space. I took out a tissue with my left hand, eliminating it from my table into the canister adjacent to me. I then positioned the receptacle away from me and fortunate for me, I had hand sanitizer which I used to wipe the table and my hands prior to returning to perusing on the PC.

That wasn't sufficient, he called me into his office and cause me to sit with him past available time. Sitting idle yet cleaning the wine stains on the dividers and cleaning those on the floors. At the point when I was done, he made me go to the café around the workplace and got him a pack of pasta with meatballs.

He ate it, gazing at me and not welcoming me. He just provided me with a container of water and a cereal bar to eat assuming I was ravenous. He kept me in the workplace with him till 10 PM, figuring out papers and searching for a document which in the end wasn't important.

I took intermittent looks at him, thinking in my mind on the off chance that I ought to recruit an expert sharpshooter to dispose of him or to approach him in a medication issue to get him away from me. It was abnormal I had these considerations knowing I'm not skilled and it was the principal I had contemplations like that. That plainly shows the amount I hate this man before me.

"It's past 9pm how are you going to get back home?"

"Take the transport."

"It's unreliable, I will take you home." I was dumbfounded when those words left his mouth and much to my shock the purpose behind it. Carlos caused me to sit in his vehicle, driving me to the intersection of my hood and drove away, letting me know he will see me at work tomorrow.

How can he hope to see me at work tomorrow when he has left me at a perilous point in my hood? I figured out how to stroll to my place of refuge, ignoring my shoulders now and again to ensure nobody was following me till I got home.

Carlos has figured out how to mix in me an inclination, I at no point ever imagined I'll have for anyone. Disdain, I disdain him for everything need he's done to me today, the most obviously terrible part is leaving me at the intersection. I wept late into the night, thinking how I've merited a manager like him in my life.

What's going on did I at any point do anything? Can't he at least show a little kindness, if I was attacked or cruelly injured by those psychos wandering my area during evening time? He shows at least a bit of kindness, everybody has. You simply don't have a place in there.

Chapter Seven

Carlos's POV

I had the snapshot of my life yesterday, laughing inside me and without holding back when nobody was near. I was exhausted as of now with the work at the workplace and chose to bring Sofia over however it was my first authority day at the workplace.

How about we simply say, I utilized Sofia to get to Ann, to annoy her since she's chosen to stayed unaffected by the entirety of my shenanigans to inspire her to leave.

I sent her to the shopping center to get me a particular chocolate and wine, declining to give her cash for a taxi a while later. I didn't miss the slight annoyance in her eyes which she immediately concealed and went out to do my offering.

Sofia came over, resembling an enchantress, an advanced Cleopatra, wearing a transparent dress which emphasized her bends. Her radiant red strap was on full presentation in her dress, making it difficult for me to focus.

I had no goals of laying my hands on her here in my office, perhaps some place yet not here and not today. I've had enough of her for now. She got on my laps, giving all her enticement abilities a shot me to get me to...you know to do that thing to her.

I was so feeling better when Valentina thumped and entered the workplace. Letting me out of the allurement I was in. Sofia evaluated her, looking all desirous at her as Valentina gave me the gift. I chuckled inside me; I truly can't comprehend this frailty of young ladies around one another. For her situation it's pointless, my collaborator couldn't measure up to her. Sofia is more tasteful and engaging than her and I don't get this superfluous desire and on second thought, would she say she is getting tenacious and possessive as of now? On the off chance that she is, I will put her on the principal trip out of my life, that is the reason I don't do connections.

I can't consolidate a tenacious companion with advantage and work in case they occupy me now that I'm manager here. To bother Valentina, I kissed Sofia who invited my lips on hers joyously. It angered me the more, here I am attempting to bother her just to do something I never need to do.

Valentina, yes that is the means by which I call her. I can't force myself to call her Isabella, it helps me to remember my crush at Antonia' congregation who I really want to go search for. She saw us, disturbed with what we were doing, more like what Sofia was doing. She left my office making gaging commotions. Might it be said that we were that gross kissing before her?

Like she can improve. I got Sofia off my lap, murmuring to her to give me her strap. I lied it was extremely hot and I really wanted it to help me to remember her.

It took everything in me not to disgust taking more time for her. I realize we carried out the thing earlier today, then I was in the mind-set for it yet presently, no I'm not and she's getting tenacious as well. That is an all-out switch off for me. "For what reason don't I see you off, I have a significant gathering at present." I lied again to get her out of my office and assuming conceivable out of my life.

She hesitantly concurred, letting me know she will see me this evening and I ought to keep my entryway, open. Like I will, I didn't. I accompanied her out fretfully, I was unable to hold on to attempt my next trick on Valentina.

"Arrange off this." She was being her PC doing God knows what. I was enticed to see what got her so stuck to the PC she didn't raise her head to recognize us when we were going out.

This time around, I got the response I needed. Her face was distorted in disdain, gazing at the strap I purposefully tossed on her table. She then, at that point, checked out at me with a pissed face. I gave her an egotistical grin and left to my office. Job well done, congrats Carlos on your first achievement! That wasn't all the very thing that I had for her for yesterday. I called her into my office and made her clean the wine I sprinkled deliberately on the divider and poured on the floor. Later sending her to get me food and when I was tired, I made her sort all through documents. Requesting for a specific document I knew was pointless however she didn't.

She did all that without resentment. At this point I was worn out and expected to return home for a loosening up shower. I asked her how she planned to return home line which she answered, the transport.

I really felt terrible for her keeping her in the workplace this late so I proposed to drive her home.

She was shocked however consented to riding with me.

We were at an intersection I have no clue off and chosen to dump her here. You know just to meddle with her one final time for the afternoon. There was a look of dread all over that got me frightened however at that point I was at that point coming and was too apathetic to even consider returning to her. I drove away yesterday feeling terrible inside me for unloading her there at that time when it was a direct result of me that she was returning home that late.

I mean on setting things right by implication to her today. Shockingly, she came to work sooner than yesterday and had previously sent my cup of articulation to my work area before I even got to inquire.

Coffee isn't my number one, I needed to manage with that yesterday and she presently believes it's my first. I shook my head at the recollections of yesterday, returning to the papers before me. I need to wrap up this arrangement and continue on to the following, to accomplish that I really want to set up a lunch meeting with Mr. Benjamin this evening. I dialed Valentina's office telephone and she got on the main ring. "Fix a booking for two at the Japanese café downtown for Mr. Benjamin and I." "OK sir, something else?"

"Better believe it get into my office." I need to direct an email for her to ship off our most recent client and furthermore make her short me on the objectives during the current month. My dad neglected to do so and is currently tasting on a martini with my mom at one of our ocean side houses in Greece. He needed severely to go get-away with my mom for that reason he was in rush to inspire me to take over with the reason of demonstrating my proficiency.

"I'm prepared sir." Valentina remained before me. Unwittingly, I evaluated her appearance. Is it safe to say that i was visually impaired that large number of times I came here and yesterday not to perceive how thick and extraordinary her body is? I more likely than not been dazed by my self-importance this while.

She was in a skirt and a turtle neck top with a coat. The skirt was so close, it featured and emphasized her executioner bends. Disregard Sofia's body, hers is thick and really engaging. Valentina made a sound as if to speak, moving awkwardly under my evaluating eyes. "You advised me to come in here, sir."

"Indeed, compose this transcription and email it to Chopra designing." I directed my desire to her. She was so effective she completed in minutes, prepared for my next task. "What are the aims for this month?"

"They're many, so which of them sir? With regards to organization, efficiency or what?"

"All."

Chapter Eight

Isabella's POV

I've been working under Satan himself a few months currently, near a year and I should say, it's been only hellfire. I'm shocked I am as yet alive after all need; he's put me through and haven't presented my acquiescence letter. He gives me no decision to do that.

Making me address task upon task, walk rapidly in my heels to finish his day-to-day tasks like we're in metro surfers where there's another undertaking consistently. I've been only productive in my work. Getting him some expresso from my number one coffeehouse each day, read his timetable to him like he educated me to, fax and send messages and gifts to whoever he wishes. I additionally reserve a spot at cafés for conferences as well as delight with that woman he sucked her face in his office.

The woman hasn't quit coming here since that day and whenever she's near, he flies off the handle, compelling me to rationalize for his sake. She doesn't hear any of it, raging into his office notwithstanding my fights.

I'm cheerful she's being a thistle in his tissue like how he makes me endure. Aside the workplace work, he has called me on in excess of five events to his home with various reasons like clockwork. Once I got so pissed, I almost smacked his hands when he messaged me saying it's critical, I come over just to arrive for him to let me know he had failed to remember what he maintains that me should do. I left and was gotten back to again three continuous times till he recollected that he believed me should get him Chinese from his number1 eatery.

I return home consistently at 9pm to my family since he has broadened my functioning hours till then and has expanded my compensation so I barely grumble. I return home so worn out, I barely eat and rather hit the sack, once in a while neglecting to scrub down.

It's all worth the effort in the end since this compensation raise has assisted me with moving my family into a less hazardous and ideal area not such a long way from my work environment.

There's this celebration coming up in about fourteen days' time which will be coordinated by our organization for a noble cause. For me it's an all-out exercise in futility, it's just a road for these high cultural individuals to focus on their abundance our countenances all for the sake of aiding the poor.

I haven't been to one since I began working here. I just get to watch the features of the recordings they take on TV and it's a simple as that. I even don't have any desire to go. I'll be exhausted siting there, stand by listening to them yak endlessly about their costly way of life. It would be more productive, being home in bed with a major container of frozen yogurt and treats, watching films with my child sister, Fabian. It might in fact be a sissy holding time.

"Have you got the scene for the celebration booked?" Mr. Carlos asked me tapping on his telephone next to me in his Ferrari, while heading to work.

I ride with him to work days he really wants me for a significant task toward the beginning of the day or days he's feeling great like today. He grinned at me when I entered the vehicle. He has an excellent grin and have to grin more. I almost told him however stayed silent and turned away in the wake of bringing it back. "Indeed, and arrangements for the occasions have begun toward the beginning of today."

"How could you know?" He asked again as yet composing on his telephone.

"I requested that they call me assuming they start in the event that there are changes to be made before they begin."

"That is ideal, give me any clues assuming there's any new turns of events."

I'm amazed hearing that remark from him. He never lauds me for any beneficial thing I do. It's generally alright, you can improve, you need to learn and stop the prior ways. Like he can endure a day without me close by. I was down with cramps a few days prior, that day he spammed my telephone with message requesting that me what do, how and when to do thing I would have done assuming I were near.

He grumbled the following day, annoying endlessly I ought to at no point ever skip work in the future. I made them work extra and covering my poo, making him resemble an insane person, going around to finish things. He began treating me somewhat better, returning to his old self now and again to keep an eye on me so I get more solid like he said.

"Hello dear my child, I miss you so much." He told whoever was on the line when he picked the call. His tone isn't similar to the one he utilizes around me. This one is delicate and brimming with love towards the individual he's talking. I took a glance at his face to see him grinning and talking.

For what reason might he at any point have that equivalent face when he converses with me if not regularly at minimum at times. I'm fed up with the stone hard articulations he gives me generally when he isn't seeming as though he's perusing me, a pleasant one wouldn't do any harm. "We should see this evening and make together for period we have not seen."

To compensate for lost times? What number of sex pals does he have? I know somewhere around four of them since I began working with him, they're so bombastic and ratchet, I can't help thinking about how he tolerates them. That make up he's discussing is a long-drawn-out evening of hot in the middle of the legs issues with the woman he's taking to. I've discovered him carrying out the thing twice at his home to know that is what he implied. I would have rather not snooped on his discussion. It's troublesome not to do so considering I'm right alongside him.

Murmuring, I likewise take out my telephone, not to settle on a decision as is he. I busied myself looking at my feed. It's more intriguing than standing by listening to my manager talk about his dreadful existence with his attractive pal at the present time, Ewwwwww.

Carlos's POV

Valentina has substantiated herself deserving of a raise of compensation in my eyes these months. She's been taking care of her business proficiently, exceeding everyone's expectations to satisfy me and keep her work. As the days went by, the similitudes among her and Isabella continued to get slender and slender. They look such a lot of the same which has made me take an incredible getting a kick out of the chance to an absent Valentina who considers me to be only her chief. Times she's not watching, I take a gander at her intently, interpreting in the event that they are similar individuals and whenever, I feel they are nevertheless I can't force myself to taking a gander at her and expand the sentiments I have for Isabella to her.

It resembles I'm undermining her despite the fact that we've never met and talked face to face. She's a mysterious sanctuary in my heart that I'm revering till I get to see her. Till now, I need to keep an expert connection with Valentina and make an honest effort to treat her right, basically for the similarity among her and my mystery love, Isabella. I've not had the option to search for her such an extremely long time, considering my bustling timetables and if I'm not mistaken, she had passed on her neighborhood to elsewhere I'm yet to track.

I'm shocked she's didn't stop regardless of the relative multitude of mean things I put her through fully intent on inspiring her to leave. I'm dazzled with her typical office works and her late night works to which I gave her a raise. She basically expressed gratitude toward me the day I told her; however, I could see such a lot of appreciation in her eyes, which made my heart melt. I for once felt in my life I've done something commendable, something that couldn't measure up to the numerous causes I've done.

Discussing noble cause, our organization is putting together an occasion in about fourteen days' time to help the less special in our area of the city as well as in nations living in wretched neediness in Asia, Africa and even Europe. It's so wide, I confided in nobody to put together it than Valentina. She's demonstrated her effectiveness, unwavering quality and commitment to our organization. I see it's a chance for her to go past her restricted obstruction and further develop her abilities more. Up until this point I'm dazzled with everything that she said to me about work starting today. I needed to converse with her all the more yet Antonia, who had been out of the country for a month presently called, frustrating me from taking part in a discussion with her.

She spoke relentless about how she misses me and can hardly wait to see me. I needed to give her desire in case she kills me, I'm going make Valentina book a reservation for us at a rich Italian café in Manhattan perhaps. I'm unsure, I'll advise her to make it, that is her work as my right hand no doubt.

We got to the organization, escaping the vehicle and strolling to the gathering like each day. Valentina had my attaché over her shoulders as she took a stab at adjusting the heap of books in her grasp. I was enticed to help her as a human seeing her going through that trouble. Right when I chose to, a woman from no place wearing a dress excessively scanty for work came towards me, grinning bashfully yet intense enough to rake my body with her eyes and when she was fulfilled, licked her lips like it was dribbling wet with chocolate syrup.

"Good morning sir, license me to assist you with these." She extended forward her hands towards mine, endeavoring to take my telephone and filtered water in them. Simultaneously, her boobs crapped out practically tumbling from where they belonged.

She was irritating me today with her modest alluring jokes. What disturbs me the most is her bosom aren't firm, they were hang and battling frantically to stay firm in her chest. "The one in particular who needs assistance here is you, go find a boob line of work, perhaps then I should seriously think about taking a gander at you." I told her in an exhausted tone, checking the time, "you've burned through great minutes of mine and her time, take those books from my aide and drop them in her office."

Valentina challenged my request with her eyes to me. I glared at her which made her reluctantly hand the books to miss drooped boobs. "Try not to take the elevator, exercise your legs using the staircase, I'm seeing you." I then, at that point, exited, with her and Valentina left, I however didn't miss the stare and threatening glare she gave my aide. Mnh botch number two today, she's in for the most terrible day of her life.

I grinned evilly to myself, realizing I will be my insidious self today and after I'm done, I don't know she will at any point attempt to encounter me. That will send the message across to those ladies in the workplace who have and need to give their scandalous things a shot me. Perhaps before long, I would need to get a limiting request against every one of them except for Valentina. Assuming I incorporate her, I'll be a dead meat. I can't most recent daily without seeing her face and her close by not as a sweetheart but rather as an aide. These times she's worked with me has made me so reliant upon her and I can in a real sense don't do anything without she being involved. She's the best colleague anybody will at any point get and assuming I'm to leave this corporate world, I'll doubtlessly drag her alongside me and obviously I won't tell her that. She will get more certain and glad.

Chapter Nine

Carlos's POV

The supper with Antonia was a complete calamity. Every one of the courses of action for it were finished by Valentina who forgot about nothing, except for Sofia who I ought to have advised her to give her the impression we were out on a business trip.

Antonia and I were at the eatery destroying and visiting enthusiastically and constant as she filled me in what happened whiles she was away for a month in Italy, my nation of origin and every one of her sexual adventures, I would have rather not heard.

It's not actually the most pleasant, standing by listening to your dearest companion inform you concerning their sexual coexistence and interest. She was at a section where she was informing me regarding one Italian person of African beginning, she met who she believes she will settle down with not in marriage when Sofia swaggered to our table, presumptuously and irately.

She blamed me for going behind her back with a sexually transmitted disease Barbie doll like Antonia and she was the justification for why I never gotten back to her or even answered her messages. You know young ladies and how they disdain being offended, Antonia was infuriated at the ridiculous allegations and abuses tossed at her and got up from her seat and sent a hot slap to the cheeks of Sofia, making an imprint on it.

Sofia fought back to the outrage of Antonia and the two ladies hurled abuses, slaps and smacks to one another. I was unable to stand it and separated them which left me with a bruised eye after Sofia hit my eye with her heel when she held back nothing.

Tragically for us, the eatery being referred to is a rich one disparaged by VIPs so there will undoubtedly be paparazzi and they heard about the thing was going on, took pictures and recordings of the battle and everything, posting it afterwards.

Mine and Antonia' picture are in question right now as a result of a dumb mix-up on my part for engaging with Sofia in any case. Her director and family have chosen to sue Sofia and her administration for every one of the harms caused to their girl. For my purposes, I will deliberately ignore it in spite of my folks contradicting my choice. I know serene, they will take care of business. I simply believe that this entire dramatization should vanish suddenly, recording a claim against her is simply going to entangle things.

Valentina helped me a ton as well. She made an official statement for my sake, coming clean and justifying me from the public eyes. The show created a ruckus in my fan base with a large number of them agreeing with my position and one other people who shot me for my way of behaving per what the media put out there are currently posting and sending me messages of how sorry they are and stuffs.

Recently, I posted interestingly since the occurrence, expressing gratitude toward every one of my fans for their help and advised them not to accept all that they hear or say and shouldn't bounce into ends without knowing the genuine side of the story. It was all gratitude to Valentina who steadily requested that I do that and it's been good.

I've been at home for seven days, working from my concentrate all things considered and dealing with this bruised eye for it to mend appropriately and on schedule for me to have the option to go to the affair. My folks will be available yet it wouldn't be a decent impression not to show. I'm the acting President now and my presence is incredibly required there.

I've left Valentina responsible for the workplace undertakings until further notice at home, alluding to me bargains which are of farthest significance. Fortunately, the dramatization didn't influence the business and every one of our clients were steady all through. I know it's their approach to demonstrating their faithfulness to us and a road for them to get all the help both monetarily and in fact.

"Sir, Mr. Matias is hanging on, on the call ask if he could stop for a short conversation with you." Valentina turned upward from the PC, stretching to give me the iPad. I called her to my home to brief me on everything occurring at the workplace, made her cook which she wouldn't fret and this moment she's reaching my fashioner on my outfit for the celebration.

I grabbed the iPad from her, extraordinarily disturbed at the irritation. The bruised eye is as yet noticeable and I won't be seen with it till it's a mended at this point this bitch of a client is requesting for a video call. "What do you need Matias?"

I paid attention to anything he needed to say till he was done and gave him my last word before abruptly hanging up, discarding the cushion not caring the least in the event that it ruins. She gave me a bad look, staring toward the headrest on the inlay floor. "What? Try not to see me like I've discarded diamonds. I have all the cash on the planet to supplant that crap, return to your work."

"Sorry sir."

"Sorry for yourself." She's an extraordinary representative yet in some cases her looks can kill and make you anxious. Continuously a holier than thou and doesn't extra me brief teaching me what is good and bad and about how individuals wish they had what I discard and give no significance to. I stood up, going to my room bothered by the call and how she took a gander at me a while later. I needn't bother with her seeing me like that this moment, there are more significant stuffs and one is getting Antonia to go with me to the function as my date after so much dramatization. I simply trust it won't ruin something we've been doing since I can recollect.

Isabella's POV

Adding the last contacts to the supper I prepared, I cleaned up and evaporated them prior to going to Mr Santiago's space to call him for supper. I won't eat here with him today, my mum necessities me at home to assist her with something she hasn't told me yet.

I thumped on the entryway, entering in the wake of hearing come in. He sat on his bed, shirtless with his telephone close by and licking his lips as he watched whatever was playing on his telephone. "Sir please the supper is ready."

I told him, swallowing down spit. The perspective on him shirtless is very upsetting truth be told, it's giving me a shivering sensation, I would rather not entertain.

He probably saw me gazing and being awkward by his shirtless stone hard and manly chest since he got up from his bed, throwing the telephone away as he did the iPad and walked around me, never looking away from me. "For what reason do I really want that, when I have a full feast just before me." He said, following his fingers on my exposed skin, making goosebumps flood my skin, his touch is giving me shivering sensations as well. He brought his head down to my neck, fanning it with his breath and run his fingers all over it. "This dinner is deluxe and I would prefer to hangout in the instant and enjoy it."

This isn't great Isabella, accomplish something before it goes crazy. His words and fingers are annoying me in hot ways. This is so bad; I can't cause him to accomplish something we both will lament the following moment. "Uhm Sir, kindly stop."

He quit fanning my cheeks yet didn't quit running his fingers on my neck and raised his go to look at me without flinching briefly, "Stop what? It isn't like you wouldn't need me in the middle of your legs right now." What? Is this all what he needs to do? "I wouldn't need you or anybody besides." I mumbled to him creeping away from him.

He rushed to snatch me by the wrist and pulled me towards him, "spare me the deception talk, you women are no different either way, modest whores. You're no less, I bet you fantasize about me when you rest. I found you gazing at me some time prior, concede that you need me."

I opened my mouth in shock, hearing those words leaving his mouth. It was so modest and there once more, I wasn't astonished hearing it from him yet for him to call me that, I won't endure him affronting me and it I'm not to call me a person or thing. "How can you even try to call me that! Dislike those bold ladies out there who don't pass up on an opportunity to give themselves wholeheartedly to you in view of your attractive features and cash. FYI there are young ladies like us out there who give no hoot to that."

"Can you just fucking stop this holier than thou attitude, I know it's a way to make me accept dislike them, whereas I am the main thing you need. Concede you need me yet don't realize how. Don't stress, I'll make it less simple for you." He winked at me, drawing nearer to me and attempting to go after my hand.

I stepped back with tears overflowing my eyes. I was unable to accept he considers me like that, a prostitute? A bed hotter? Gosh! "I'm frustrated with myself for tolerating a man as nauseating as you with an idiotic and modest attitude. Think of me as an ex representative reason from this evening, I quit this entire crap you call work." I spat the words like they were toxin at him and take off from his room, down the trip of stairs.

I express gratitude toward God I didn't trip with the speed at which I run down them and grabbed my sack from the parlor lounge chair and out the entryway as quick as possible.

Karma isn't my ally today of the entire days, it was coming down hard as I escaped his home into the roads. There wasn't a single vehicle to be seen and I was the just being on the road at this moment. I strolled through the downpour, splashing my garments and concealing the tears I'm shedding. I knew about who he was before I begun working for him. How idiotic of me to think a stone hearted and self-important man like him can at any point change. I thought those grins he gave me and little fondness he displayed towards me were authentic and that he has improved however no. He was as yet his jerky self, no regret at all for his moronic way of behaving. I acclaim myself for facing him today and daring to stop however my whole occupation and that of my family rely upon my compensation. It's a terrible decision yet no decision is awful when you take more time to safeguard your own poise and deserve admiration for you. I'll get another line of work some way or another, regardless of whether wandering through this city to get one, I will.

Chapter Ten

Isabella's POV

My caution went off uproariously and annoyingly making me jerk up from my rest and hit my head against my headrest. Moronic morning timer, I rub my head and hit the clock prior to switching it off. The aggravation has made me completely alert, taking a gander at the time, it's 6:00 am. It's past my standard awakening time, was I so worn out I dozed in?

I jumped up and immediately went into the restroom to carry out my morning responsibility in record time with the expectations of getting to early work. It was the point at which I had completed washing and dried myself and I was searching for an outfit to wear that I recalled that, I quit my place of employment yesterday.

The occasions of yesterday currently turned out to be straight from the time that fallen angel himself pulled that trick on me to his words and my reprisal and to me leaving his home into the cold downpour and when I dropped in the road.

I was feeling better and terrified all together, awakening to musky cologne and arms of a wonderful man in a house that wasn't comfortable. I sniffled and grasped my head when he asked about my wellbeing. My head was pounding with a migraine and my nose was impeded, what I get for remaining out in the downpour.

He presented himself as Samuel Nicolas a business investor who was on his way from an excursion for work when he saw me dropped in the downpour in the road. He lovingly blew up at me not to at any point rehash that since it wasn't great and he needed to call a specialist to investigate me to ensure I was okay.

I expressed gratitude toward him for his consideration and notwithstanding my fights, he acquired me back home new tracksuit pants and a hoodie, to safeguard me from the virus. He took my number, letting me know he will call to investigate me till I improve. I grinned at him and becoming flushed when he let me know pretty young ladies don't need to become ill, it causes the fine young men to feel terrible, amusing him.

Discussing Satan, he just sent me a message.

Nicolas: I trust your morning is all around as brilliant as your astonishing grin, Good morning pretty love and how are you getting along today?

Me: Great morning Nicolas, I'm much better today and yourself?

AJ: I'm fine if you are

Me: Say thanks to God, I realize I said this yesterday however I'm obliged to say it once more. Many thanks for your assistance yesterday, I don't where I would have been without you. God favor you.

Nicolas: Nah relax, it's anything but nothing to joke about. I was delighted to be of help to a lovely refined you. Might I at any point take more time to lunch throughout your break?

Me: I don't work yet certain.

Nicolas: according to your garments yesterday, you work so for what reason would you say you are letting me know you don't?

Me: I used to, I quit before you tracked down me.

Nicolas: Then, at that point, it's my big chance to shine, I end up requiring a temp for certain months. Perhaps you right?

Me: I'll consider it, see you at lunch Igtg.

Nicolas: okay.... your name?

Me: my terrible, I'm Valentina.

Nicolas: lovely name for an excellent young lady

I grinned and locked my telephone, putting it on my bed prior to connecting for shorts and a tee. I took my telephone from the bed and stuffed it in my pocket as I left my room.

Fabian was in her room preparing for school when I peeped into her Manuel Couture, that is the very thing she calls it. After a few supplications and pup eyes, I permitted her enliven it to her own taste and inclination, she wound up making it resemble a style symbol's room. Her dividers were put with arrangements and pictures of Antonia Manuel Juan, her unsurpassed style goddess and her shelves were fixed with magazines and newspaper articles of her. Her room resembles a sanctuary of Antonia, and that wouldn't shock me at all assuming she one day meets her. There's gossip she goes to our congregation however I don't how genuine it is, never seen her with my own eyes around there previously.

I moved in an opposite direction from her room and walked around the lounge. Mother was situated on the sofa, perusing the morning's paper and tasting her number one refreshment, tea. She momentarily gazed upward from the paper and tended to me, "great morning heavenly messenger, how are you feeling?"

"I'm extraordinary mum and you?" I asked her, turning on the television. I'm not exactly hungry earlier today, I've completely lost my hunger with what happened yesterday and about that, I don't figure I can tell my mom. She will stress and figure profoundly over how we will get by and assuming we will continue to live which can set off a stroke or a   hypertension.

"I'm fine as well, for what reason would you confirm or deny that you are dressed for work yet? Time's slipping away."

"I phoned in wiped out working, my supervisor has allowed me a few days off." I considered cautiously prior to proclaiming that falsehood and how it ought to never be found out.

"He's a good man to have given you some days off and in addition today." Mother said and smiled at me. I quietly heaved and feigned exacerbation, if by some stroke of good luck, she knew who she was discussing and alluding to as a pleasant man. He isn't and can never be, he's the contrary meaning of decent, a reasonable meaning of a terrible individual.

For what reason did I need to work under him? Furthermore, for what reason did I at any point need to tolerate him this while? Yesterday was the straw that broke the camel's back and I'm never going to set my foot into his office regardless of whether I'm offered huge number of dollars to work for him again.

I want to get my butt up from this love seat and get into my room, change into new and formal garments and go out there to look for a task if I have any desire to cover my falsehood and ensure it's rarely out in the open.

My mom will be dampen to realize I misled her about something actually that genuine, I would rather not start with Fabian as well. I can't tolerate seeing her miserable face and attempting to work really hard to help us in her own little manner. I'm the oldest, I should do that and not her, all I need is for her to zero in on her schooling and get a superior degree later on. I moaned and got up from my seat and went into the kitchen to plan breakfast for Fabian and mother before I go out looking for a task. We were out of food and subsequent to scanning the cupboards for quite a while, I found a container of oat cornflakes and milk which will keep going for now and tomorrow. I've given careful consideration to go shopping for food later in the day with the little left of my reserve funds I utilized in getting us this house. There was compelling reason need to broil eggs or bacon, I put the cornflakes and milk on the island kitchen and went to my room.

I didn't have a lot of garments so I changed into a pants and hoodie, integrating my hair with a pig tail on my head and snatched my side pack from the coat rack and swung it around my shoulder.

I didn't annoy myself examining the mirror. I look fine and dandy, I've worn these garments so often to know how I examine them. I put on my boots and drew out my telephone subsequent to hearing it buzz in my sack.

There was a text from Jay inquiring as to whether I'm on my way in light of the fact that the manager was in and was requesting for me. I feigned exacerbation and sent him an answer, phoning in debilitated and stuffed my telephone into my pocket as I opened the front entryway.

I hollered, saying farewell to my mum carelessly and strolled to the asphalt before our home. I remained there looking from left to right, considering where to go first. The left will take more time to my organization and other fruitful ones and the right will take more time to the amusement part of our little city where the strip clubs, typical clubs, theaters, computer game stores and artful dance school are.

I took the left, I will walk pass the organization and not care how it look but rather go take a shot at the telecom organization and material organization around. Or on the other hand perhaps I can consider Nicolas's proposition, who can say for sure what today has for me? Just the man up there. I raised my head to gaze at the sky, offering a quiet petition to God to favor me today and make me fruitful as I continued looking for a task.

I then, at that point, took the transport, sitting discreetly to myself and stayed out of other people's affairs till I landed at the telecom organization. Taking in and out, I murmured to myself, "Ruler God as we examined" and assembled all the certainty, I had as I advanced toward the gathering.

Part Eleven

Isabella's POV

I lethargically rub my eyes and yawn, awakening from bed. My quest for a task yesterday, at first wasn't looking encouraging. I was skipped from the telecom organization and the materials as well, causing me to lose the desire for finding a new line of work. I meandered erratically around for a really long time till I went over an immense structure with an expansive engraving, Chapman Hardware.

I effortlessly recognized it as the renowned hardware organization that was known in each family throughout recent decades, creating quality and reasonable gadgets for the many years now.

I came to later figure out the organization was possessed by Samuel when I was approached to see the chief. You could envision the amazement all over, interacting with the very individual who extended to me an employment opportunity and saved my life as well. He would have rather not talked with me yet recruit me straight up.

I felt it wasn't correct, I ought to get business in light of my abilities and after much cajoling, he allowed me a meeting with a couple of associates for it not the one-sided and yass! It all made sense to me.

I'm currently going to be Nicolas's partner for quite a while till his long-lasting one gets back from her a half year leave and thereafter move to another office. The occupation has adaptable terms, I get a compensation not so high as my previous one but rather adequate to cause us to make due and I can enjoy some time off whenever I need to. It accompanies free protection and motivation rewards and excursions to any nation of my decision with my family, isn't excessively grand?

I'll make certain to go with my mom and Fabian to the Caribbean one summer break and partake in the bright sea shores. For the time being, I need to get up from my rest and plan for the supper I have with Nicolas in an hour.

After our lunch yesterday, he let me know he appreciated it and would need to rehash it with me tomorrow. I acknowledged in the wake of inquiring as to whether he had an exceptional woman in his life to which he answered with a no. I definitely approved of it as long as no woman will come towards me and assault me like Mr. Carlos's model sweetheart did to Antonia.

It's a disgrace he was outlined for something which wasn't accurate and Antonia needed to languish the most over his activities. It will show him next time not to play with individuals since he is the boss.

Feigning exacerbation, I went into my washroom and clean up. I've snoozed and there's just an hour left. Express gratitude toward God I'm not one to keep long in sprucing up and I don't claim a lot of supper dresses so I'll be great to in picking one out of the two I have. That is one benefit of claiming less garments, no time squandering and migraine in getting the right one.

I was before my wardrobe, looking for the dresses when Fabian burst into my room, grinning and squirming her foreheads at me. She drooped her thick body on my bed and turned towards me, "mum said you eat with your supervisor this evening, since when did both of you become... you know?"

"There's nothing happening between us. It's a cordial supper, not much so how about you get your butt up and help me over here. I don't know which to wear, either?" I asked, spreading the dresses out so that her might be able to see. She's the fashionista between we two sisters so she has to assist me with nailing it right this evening and look adequate. I can't be resembling a cartoon and follow a Luis like Nicolas, an attractive and running Greek god to an eminent café, it's not great for the picture, they say.

"Wear the blue, it draws out your variety most and match it with the heels I got you for your birthday last year." She told me tossing me the dress. I got it in my grasp and gazed at it for at some point, it's the dress out of the two that I don't actually feel great wearing. It's tight, knee length and draws out my bends that I don't need anybody seeing and enticing men, we should confront realities, my body is what others pay cash to get and I especially don't adore parading it. It causes superfluous consideration from the other gender. I must choose between limited options since my fashionista sister of a beautician picked it for me, applying salve on my body and getting into undies, I took my bra and endeavored to put it on when Fabian's voice halted me. "You needn't bother with a bra sister."

"It's a strapless bra, it won't show."

"Your costume is a salacious collar neck which does not need a bra." She facepalmed and feigned exacerbation decisively. "All sensible miss fashionista." I said in a teasing voice, she kept feigning exacerbation at me as she stood up from the bed and move to my shoe rack.

I looked as she fished out the Valeria warrior lower leg wrap heels, she gifted me with.

"Since your dress has a cut that isn't excessively profound, these heels will be best for you." She went into my bag this time around and took out a straightforward layered arm band, "something to clean up your outfit, you needn't bother with a neckband the bridle neck is an over-the-top show as of now."

I expanded at her, taking the arm band from her. I realized Fabian was a style darling however not to this great to know what's right and ideal for a dress or an outfit. Amazing! I took a gander at my appearance in the mirror and I was so enamored with it, she has styled me so right, I seem as though I'm going to an elegant design show. I'm looking so extravagant dislike my bank Tomas at the present time. "Many thanks love, I recommend you seek after a style course cause this ability can't go to squander."

"I was conceived prepared for the design world sister yet the main issue is, could we at any point bear the cost of me going to a style school in this cutting-edge US? You realize I can't go to only any junior college for it." Her eyes lost the flicker in them as she plunked down and broke into tears.

She has a point however, going to a design school is definitely not something simple particularly for individuals like us who're attempting to earn enough to get by. It's costly however worth the effort. Seeing her plunking down there and being miserable got me miserable as well, on the off chance that that is what she needs, it's my right as an older sister to do as such. We need to seek after what our hearts needs regardless, that is called energy. "Take a glimpse at me Gwendolyn, in the event that I'm to slave myself to work every one of the long stretches of my life only for you to go to A rundown style school for you to become who you want to be, child sister, I will without reconsidering. So clear that misery off of your face and grin more, it's our main sun in these dull days of our lives."

"Thank you, kindly Isabella, I don't have any idea what we would have managed without you in our lives." She flung her arms around me, maneuvering me into an embrace, "I love you definitely and I vow to make you and mum glad for me."

"I don't question that child; I realize you will and I love you beyond what you can imagine me." We parted from our sissy embrace, I grinned at her and cleaned her face with the rear of my hand, "you look terrible when you cry Fabian." I expressed that to ease up the state of mind and it sure did. She laughed and cleared away the little hints of detaches from her face, "I realize I know, that why I barely cry. Presently go, you would rather not keep Mr. Santiago hanging tight for him to turn around into mean boss."

"Better believe it right, I'll see you this evening in the event that you ain't snoozing when I get back." Much to your dismay I never again work for him. I disdain that I'm deceiving them yet I must choose between limited options considering the conditions that drove me to stop. Perhaps I can come clean with them since I have a new position with the Chapmans.

"You see, you smash him with your beauty Isabella." She sparkled at me and grinned, giving me my telephone and tote bag. I shook my head and shut the way to my room, passing on her in there to utilize my old PC to watch style recordings, that is the very thing that she generally does.

I took as much time as necessary, using the stairwell in case I fall in these heels. It's somewhat elusive and I implore I endure this night without stumbling and shaming myself out in the open. On the off chance that I do I'm most likely going to petition God for the ground to open up and swallow me.

The entryway chime rang and I was down on schedule to open it.

Chapter Twelve

Isabella's POV

The man before me was an incredible sight. He was dressed immaculately in a light blue short Donato's shirt, featuring his conditioned strong arms and dim chino pants sticking to his legs.

He had his naval force coat threw around his shoulder and fair hair style flawlessly in a shape blur with short dreadlocks on top. I unknowingly looked at him and swallowed perceiving how attractive and masculine he was looking right presently contrasted with yesterday, I like the dreadlocks.

He found me gazing at him and grinned, making a sound as if to speak, he extended his hand towards me, "may I have the delight?"

I modestly gestured my head, "most definitely," and intertwined his hand with mine as we strolled to his vehicle, a Bugatti Chiron and get in it. His palm was delicate, warm and sweat-soaked all together and it made them keep thinking about whether he was apprehensive with this as am I.

I'm apprehensive and bashful in light of the fact that one: it's my first time going out to supper, two with a man as attractive as him and three, I couldn't say whether I was underdressed or overdressed considering he didn't let me know where precisely we were going and he hasn't commended me to facilitate this anxiety.

"I realized you were a wonder from the time I met you yet this evening, you've blown my mind. You looking flawlessly dazzling this evening Valentina." He said in a thick English articulation as though guessing what I might be thinking and contemplations and brushed his fingers against my hand as he changed hands on the wheel.

My face warmed up at the actual contact among us and the commendation, making me look hesitantly on my laps and fiddle with my fingers. "Much obliged to you Nicolas."

"Nah don't make reference to it." He waved his hand pompously, speeding up. The vehicle ride then, at that point, turned quiet, I was too modest to even consider talking and he likewise appeared as though he needed to focus more out and about before him, given the maximum velocity at which he was   driving.

The vehicle pulled up to a structure, I was confounded from the beginning seeing it resembling a café or a diner until we escaped the vehicle after he looked out for me. We strolled into the structure and on another once-over, it ended up being an extravagant café, improved to suite the flavor   of   the   rich.

It not having an engraving in front obviously demonstrates, it's not for the general population but rather the tip top, the people who can manage the cost of know their direction here like Nicolas did.

I unexpectedly dropped awkward, contrasting myself with those around. The women were wearing costly dresses, manicured hands holding wine glasses and amazing red and purple shaded lips tasting the wine and bending into a grin that didn't arrive at their eyes, the men were no special case, they generally looked great and well fitted for this sort of climate and not me.

Nicolas waved a hand before me, "hello would you say you are paying attention to me?"

"Better believe it definitely, what did you say once more?" I guess I was sleepy when I was to be checking out these wealthy people. "I asked as to whether you would agree that we pick a table here or somewhere more private."

"Uh anything as you would prefer, I'm cool with it." Anything is great with me as long as I don't get gazed from these individuals, seeing a couple of them peering toward me up.

"The very some place more private so I can have you all to myself." I become flushed at his words and laughed as well, I thoroughly concur with you on this. "Will we?"

"Yes, we will." I remembered this answer from question tags way back in secondary school and desire to use it. He drove the way to the private part of the eatery which had not many individuals there and picked a table at the corner, pulling a seat for me, "says thanks to Nicolas."

"My pleasure." He pulled a seat as well and reclined across from me, "Please accept my apologies for my quiet back in the vehicle, I simply didn't have the foggiest idea how to begin a convo with a hypnotizing elegant you." He began his hand timidly as he said the last part.

"There's compelling reason need to apologize; I was quiet as well."

"I requested we go out for dinner, because I feel it is my duty to keep you engaged till the night is north of." A waiter came to our table with a smile at us. He checked out momentarily at me then at Nicolas. "A jug of Moët Chamdon for us."

The server gestured and disappeared to present to us the Champagne. Nicolas took out his telephone for certain, minutes, composing on it and made a sound as if to speak to acquire my consideration when he was finished, "Uh sorry for utilizing my telephone, that was my mom."

"Tell me about her." I don't know what came over me to say whatever it is that I said. He looked astonished at my solicitation, most likely asking why I believed him should do that when this supper should be about us, for us to get to know one another better.

"Uhm well, Mother is the only dependable person, I have always know at any point. Strolling her direction through a shocking union with my progression father to independently working constantly to care for my four other male kin and I through school, costly ones so far as that is concerned in Britain since she believed us should get only awesome until she met her dad, who repudiated her for experiencing passionate feelings for my dad since he was poor and a womanizer as well. They accommodated and he helped us from that point, giving us the best life and presently here I am. As yet taking care of her in everything in light of the fact that to me she is a divine being, nobody can go through what she managed without separating sooner or later however she didn't, continuously keeping her head high and being solid as far as we're concerned, at first I thought she was made of steel." He chuckled at that part absentmindedly and gone on with it, "I've made her glad for me yet I need to do it more by getting hitched very soon and settling down. I'm the main left of my kin frantic storage room to her heart who isn't hitched despite everything carrying on with the lone ranger's life." He closed his story. All through, I evaluated him as he talked, he had this yearning look all over which changed to pride as he discussed his mom and afterward trouble at the last part.

Trouble that I wish I knew a method for cleaning away for an obscure explanation. I was enticed to ask him about for what valid reason he was miserable at the last part yet figured it was touchy and individual so I left it at that and gave his hand a delicate crush which frightened him, making him look at me. Various sorts of feelings moving in his eyes until he turned away and when he turned around, they were gone, his eyes being back to their ordinary dim variety.

Samuel's POV

Sitting with Valentina in the vehicle and inverse her at the eatery this moment, is making me see ladies in an all the better light. My previous encounters with ladies haven't been awesome, ladies involving me for the cash I have as opposed to adoring me for who I'm in the end made me shut them generally out till I met her that evening in the city.

I was returning from seven days' work excursion in Russia and chose to utilize that course since it was the wardrobe to my area. I was driving at maximum velocity very much like generally when I heard a voice in my mind to dial back. I didn't actually observe it until I heard it for the subsequent time and this time around, I complied and eased back them. Simply relatively close to where I dialed back, I saw a body in the city.

I from the start mixed up it to be that of an out on the lush's road subsequent to getting squandered on liquor and chosen to drive past. Upon a more intensive take care of escaping my vehicle, I saw a lovely young lady, totally dropped in the road, wearing continuous garments.

I thought it was a trick, you know to inspire me to bring her back home and burglarize me so I investigated her pack and observed papers showing she works for Santiago vehicles. That made me convey her from the floor into my vehicle and in the end getting it wet, I wouldn't fret as long as I was saving a human.

So, running over her has made me see ladies from an alternate perspective, she is so rational, legitimate and interesting. I need to get to know her more that is the reason I requested to take her out to supper today.

I thought I had met a heavenly messenger when I remained in her doorstop at her home. Pure black unusual hair in a bun on her head, blue body con dress embracing her impeccably, stressing her inherent bends and thin hands that held the entryway open for me. Her enrapturing excellence stunned me and when I at long last gotten comfortable with myself, I had the desire to hold her hand and I did exactly that.

I was past anxious, the sensation of having a staggering like her close to me made my heart race like a long distance race, making me moronic all over the course of the time in the vehicle and I even battled inside before I had the option to converse with her after we showed up.

Her solicitation for me to educate her regarding my mom astounded me definitely. She's the above all else the women I've taken more time to ask something to that effect, the last ones were just keen on the food and the cash they will get a while later and her authentic premium in needing to hear it, captivated me the more.

I've been endlessly looking; I think I've at long last viewed as the one. The very words that were ringing in my ears as I gazed at her face in the wake of enlightening her regarding my mom and her desire to get me hitched. I shook those words away, I'm charmed okay, however isn't it too soon to think I've succumbed to her as of now? I've found out about unexplainable adoration and to me it's false. Love can't be surged that way; it takes more time to bring its actual importance out.

Valentina Isabella Romeo. I continued to rehash her name in my mind, it's a great name for a lovely woman who I wish past sky, she's the right one to bring her back home.

Chapter Thirteen

Carlos's POV

"Sei un story idiota Carlos." Alejandro, my other dearest companion, the one I trust most among my companions, became suddenly angry at me for the millionth time in Italian, the language he utilizes when he's pissed today and grabbed the glass of vodka from my hand, setting it before him. (You such a simpleton Carlos."

"Haha in this way, lo so Alejandro." I endeavored to grab the liquor from him yet bombed wretchedly. I'm toasted the center causing me to fail to keep a grip on everything even my typical self however not my faculties, I'm particularly mindful of the discussion we're having now. (I know, I know Alejandro.)

"So, you acknowledge you screwed up for sure?"

"Si." I pull at my hair in disappointment, reality truly damages and that is the way it feels at the present time. I realize I screwed up big time which had made me lose my most faithful laborer, exactly the same I gave the obligation of the organization and affair arrangements to. How I'm I going to confront my folks particularly my dad, should the affair end up being a catastrophe, a total shame to our family poise considering the quantity of first-class profiles in this country who will join in. In view of my moronic activities. (Indeed.) "Quindi fare,ammendate." I wish I knew how to do that; I would have done it instantly. I'm currently a dead meat without her in the workplace, taking care of all my necessities like the loyal worker she is. (Then, at that point, offer to set things right.)

"Non è cosi effortless perte dirlo." (No, it's not so natural as you say.)

"È efficiente e labriosa?" (She's productive and focused?)

"Si." (Yes.)

"Dedicato?" (Committed?)

"Si stupido!." I'm sincerely getting tired of his endless inquiries, I don't have the foggiest idea what he's attempting to demonstrate or how it'll settle this poop. For what reason did I at any point call him here when I realized he wouldn't check out, he's pretty much as inept as I'm. Continuously making errors and allowing our cash to pay for them. (Indeed dumb!)

"Leale?" (Steadfast?)

"Edici Bella?" (And you say excellent?)"

"Extremely." Valentina's delightful, guiltless and enthralling face comes into vision. The light spots on her cheeks bones and stout lips, gracious my! that I took looks at whenever she was close by. Indeed, even in my plastered state, I actually recall them distinctively. Extremely enticing, really awful I botched my opportunity.

"Allora scusarsi con lei e admission ammenda, lei è un groiello. Then, at that point, sarole sacoli ask for forgiveness and set things right, she is a groiello. You have perceived the amount you have been squandered since she left.)

I gesture, "Sai che sono un Ginanni, non prego." His voice hauls me out of my fantasizing of Valentina's lips, into the present, where I'm actually being addressed by this stupid companion of mine here. I wish he will leave and let me be to swallow down tons of alcohol into my system. At any rate, it will cause me to fail to remember what is happening I'm in. (You know I'm a Santiago, I don't ask.)

"Eppure sei umano, che cosa ti è vermente venuto in mente? I stayed quiet, unfit to respond to his inquiry. That is one inquiry I've remained quiet about posing, what the heck came over me? I was pissed on account of the call and Valentina's look since I discarded the iPad and left to my room, thinking it planned to get me out of that disposition however nah. My fascination or love or anything I desire to call it, with Isabella made me look at their congregation page and luckily, her presentation from that evening was caught. (However, you're human, what truly came into your psyche?)

As I watched it, I saw likeness among her and Valentina, then it was too confounding to even consider striking similitudes. There and afterward, I concluded there was just a single method for finding out, assuming genuinely the young lady I'm so stricken with is Valentina no doubt or it's simply my own deception of attempting to persuade myself they are similar individuals since they're Valeria and excellent. Definitely I have to concede Valentina's excellent, similar to my Isabella.

I realized she was preparing supper then and will before long come up to my space to call me first floor so I busied myself, looking on my telephone when I heard her thump on my entryway.

She entered, letting me know supper is prepared like I anticipated. Perhaps it was my creative mind or perhaps not however I saw her change into Isabella, then, at that point, herself, again to Isabella lastly back to herself.

It was torturing, I was unable to take it any longer. I set my strategy in motion, strolling towards her and doing something I've been significance to do, trail my fingers on her body. I cherished how she answered my touch: goosebumps and shudders!

It helped me to accomplish more and I thought twice about it. Calling her a whore, something I'm at absolutely no point ever going to total in the future. I saw red in her eyes, outrage and hurt. I was excessively profound into my inept allegation and put-downs to pull out, I looked as she broke into tears just before me. My heart broke, why I'm I excessively unforgiving towards ladies, particularly poor people? It isn't their issue and not every one of them are that way assuming Tamara my ex did that, it doesn't mean Valentina, Isabella or the rest out there would.

It was past the point of no return when regret overwhelmed me, she had proactively stopped and was out of my room and presumably out of my home and life. Until the end of time. I'd lost my best representative, the main partner who at any point faced me and set up with all my hogwash and the one who helped me such a huge amount to remember my mystery crush, Isabella.

My pride as a man, Santiago and Luis and cherished superstar didn't give me heart to go dependent upon her and ask till she pardons me. Presently here I am, becoming inebriated to fail to remember this entire thing. Liquor isn't settling it however this case, it's aiding me not recollect it. A simple indication of it makes my heart jerk, as it's doing at present.

Chapter Fourteen

Carlos's POV

"Fuck!" I murmur uproariously and discard my telephone. I can't completely accept that this is going on the present moment, today of the entire days when it's the ideal opportunity for the occasion and Antonia chose to discard me. Saying she has a crisis business and is en route to Boston as   I   speak.

I can't show up without a date close by. A female figure to make the impression I'm an all-around man and not some playboy. They say it's great for business and presently how am I going to do that?

Amalia, my freshest partner strolled into my review with a melancholy look all over. She dashed her eyes to the broke telephone on the floor and afterward back at me. My rising chest and glare gave her a more motivation to move in an opposite direction from me and not convey anything that news she has. She pardoned herself to investigate the models I requested that she book a meeting with on the off chance that Antonia bombs me and deciding by her look, it turned out poorly or it may very well be my pessimism. "Spill the goddamn crap and leave!" I barked at her, taking both my infuriation on her and getting tired of her uncertain way of behaving.

"Uh-Sir-the-"

"The what! Stop this faltering and completely finish since I realize you don't stammer while you're groaning and getting some."

"Please accept my apologies sir," she become flushed and looked downwards, "I implied the models said they can't make it, they've been reserved and the escort organization I enquired from said they're disliking the federal authorities throughout recent weeks thus can't deliver their administrations and they're extremely sorry as well, the proprietor advised me to let you know she will actually make it dependent upon you."

I heaved at that, I needn't bother with no old twat to satisfy me. I get the young ladies whenever I can with simply an applaud of my hands, they'll be at my feet doing what they know best. "Invest more effort! Is it true that you are this clumsy? Could it be said that you are attempting to let me know I'm squandering my cash in paying you only for you not to demonstrate no outcomes?"

"No sir, I did everything what I could however it's as yet unchanged. Each organization and model I contact is giving me stories, sir it resembles somebody noticeable out there is paying them to do that-"

"Close your snare, there's nobody as conspicuous as all of us in this entire city and country. Get out! You futile reason of an assistant."

"Sorry sir." She submissively bowed her head and made for the entryway.

She wasn't out of it when a thought came into my head, "Miss Grayson, put my beautician at risk for me."

"Alright sir." She truly got serious l, stretching out the telephone to me, "she's on the line sir."

"Adela, take your best stuffs and your entire group and go to this location," I stopped and fished out a record from my private cabinet, skimming through it, I told her the said address and hanged up.

Life is a success and lose issue, this evening, I have my fingers crossed as I guess how all that will end up. It's most certainly a twofold success on the off chance that my thought goes through effectively and an incredible misfortune on the off chance that it doesn't.

Chapter Fifteen

Isabella's POV

My day today was somewhat exhausting and in opposition to what I needed. I was in a real sense at home the entire day with my mom, doing nothing to the side fixing us a pleasant fair feast and sitting at the entryway patio, chatting with her. I could have done without the piece of me waiting and not being out there working really hard to get cash and mother even gave her all to get my psyche of it.

I adored the part I had an incredible quality time with my mom, enjoying each moment of this is on the grounds that when I begin working with Nicolas, I'll be occupied and may return home late relying upon his timetables.

I'm laying on my bed with Fabian close to me, stuffing our appearances with fries she brought from school. I was finished with mine and eating the frozen yogurt that accompanied the French fries,

"Uh Fabian, shift focus over to one side and take my telephone for me.

"Your telephone is next to you trying to say that so I don't get to watch Martinez and Aurelia sucking faces. Since I'm a decent young lady, imma cover my eyes." She expressed giggling at me, getting on to my   stunt.
We were watching this sappy heartfelt film on the net, two individuals who're enamored with one another however are dating others just to dispose of what they feel. They're thoroughly irritating me with their absurdity, why date another person when you have your first love as of now? They're at the part where they will share spit and being the best sister I'm, I'm requesting that Fabian look somewhere else on the grounds that she's young and this sixteen years of age sissy of mine definitely is familiar with sucking faces? Where has the world gotten to?

In my time, we had no clue on the off chance that it. Who I'm I joking? Individuals underneath her age during my days were at that point carrying out the thing, leaving them with series of exs. What a screwed up age! "Hello how could you realize they planned to do that? Who educated you?" She concealed her face from me as her face got red. Mnh this ain't great, she's done some as of now. "Uh somebody constrained himself on me and did that." "Who Fabian?" This time I was up from resting to sitting. This is a big deal, need to investigate. Nobody has the option to ruin my child sister. "Somebody from my group, a kid. He continued grinning at me and winking and on one occasion he did that to me after school. That was the day I returned home with puffy eyes. Eww it was nauseating, I lashed out and punched him in the nose, denoting his face with my nails." Damn! That was unforgiving. It wasn't really great for the kid to that to her yet it wasn't ideal for

Fabian to turn to savagery, it simply ain't correct. "He did not do well, It is better you report him than beating him. Brutality is never the right solution."

"Alright Isabella, I felt awful the following day seeing him with a swollen nose and his head hung low. From that point forward he never taken a stab at doing that to me or approaching me." She said with trouble all around her face.

"Did you know him?"

"No doubt he was my companion, a decent one who shielded me from the domineering jerks at school. I simply don't have the foggiest idea what got into him."

"Menaces? Which individuals are you discussing miss?" I said in my most harsh voice. I can't really accept that my child sister experienced tormenting in school and never tried to inform us.

"Uhm.." she's seeming as though a child discovered in the act, taking meat from soup.

I didn't be able to hearing about the domineering jerks as my mom shouted for her from ground floor. "Mother's calling you, go to her and when you get back here. You must educate me everything, perhaps after that I'll visit your school."

Fabian gestured, getting up hastily from the bed. She looked too glad to even consider leaving, which caused me to understand the seriousness of the harassing. Is it true or not that i was excessively occupied with looking for cash to miss those times she returned home with marks or weepy appearances?

I murmured and fell once again into bed. I know how it seems like to be the substitute in school, I had gone through that to be aware. My main rescuer was, my chief was an extremely kind lady who investigated the issue and authorized the offenders, making everybody my own guardians to ensure those domineering jerks never drew near to me enough to hurt me. I say thanks to God for Mrs. Mateo's life and incredible assistance back in secondary school.

Fabian returned into the room, grinning and her eyes glimmering. It was in opposition to how she was the point at which she was experiencing this room.

Following right behind her were individuals who resemble them in the design business, no big surprise Fabian is so blissful.

They pushed past her and the head of them grinned at me, "we have orders from your manager to style you this evening for the occasion." I was befuddled, Nicolas didn't make reference to there would have been an occasion at the workplace and that he planned to send individuals to my home to style me up.

The lady gave me no space to dissent, she gave me a shopping sack, shooing me into the washroom to put it on. Nicolas truly owes me a ton of clarification for this, I disdain shocks regardless of whether they're great ones. Somewhat cautioning in advance would have been valued. "Times not on our side Valentina, if it's not too much trouble, come out."

I was scarcely done putting it on. I ran out for the restroom and sat on the seat, pushed before me. This time around, a lady looking man, famously known as a cross dresser came towards me, conveying a container which ended up being a make up pack in the wake of opening it.

I stayed there not knowing what amount of time it endured as he required for his time, giving me a facial makeover. This while, one more woman sat adjacent to me, manicuring my hands making me sometimes turn away to get a new inhale of air, the fluids she's utilizing don't have the most pleasant fragrance, so sharp!

They wrapped up with their work and the manager woman herself had her spot behind me and made for my hair. I saw her take out a hair straightener utilizing it on my hair. The steam from it made me handle the seat, trusting so hard it doesn't consume me, it's the explanation I barely fix my hair and my unusual hair is difficult asf. I sit on my butt hours just to inspire it to appropriately fix. "Gosh madam, your hair is hard, it's difficult to bow even with my hair dryer." She said to me, laughing. I laughed as well, I thought I was the only one it gave issues to.

"OK so we are done, Emilliano brings the mirror. You give her the grasp; we're using up all available time here and you know how the manager detests delay and pausing." She woofed directions to her group as she peered down on her wristwatch.

I endeavored to remain to stand up yet a hand pulled me down to sit, an excellent woman gazed at me, grinning at me. Her eyes seemed as though she was fainting over me, I got her glance at me down and up, licking her lips. I'm into young men not young ladies! I needed to flawlessly tell her yet ruled against it. She drew out an adornments box and put around my neck a precious stone studded choker and matching hoops on my ear. "Well that is great."

I grinned at her, taking the grasp from the make up craftsman and slide my feet into the stiletto impact points, strolling to the mirror.

I wheezed at the appearance before me. Goodness my mom that ain't me! I can't remember me, the make up was absolutely right on track. The white plume off the shoulder mermaid dress, fitted me impeccably, complementing those bends I so don't have any desire to see at the present time. My hair has been fixed and made into a side gruff trim, sparkling impeccably with the choker.

So, I look dazzling. I'm feeling myself right now as I run my hands along the dress, I love it, it's respectable and doesn't show a lot of skin. The quill around the top is keeping any cleavage from appearing. Exactly the way in which I love my dresses! Stunning.

"Wow Isabella, you resembling sovereignty! I bet your manager will be stricken by you. He ain't gonna take his eyes way from you the smallest." Fabian who had hushed up this while screeched, whirling me around. The others in the room, gestured, concurring with her.

"Okay, okay enough of this. The manager is restlessly sitting tight for her, so my dear accompanied me." She locked her telephone and stuffed in her pocket, "you folks ought to return the van to the work, I'll be with you instantly."

I bid farewell to an invigorated Fabian who continued to pantomime blowing kisses at me till I went out, following supervisor woman to the vehicle, sitting tight for us: a smooth limousine. Mnh refinement at its ideal.

Chapter Sixteen

Isabella's POV

I was nervous all through the ride in the limo and needed to demand for a glass of water to assist with quieting me down. I guessing's really going to happen this evening and where we're truly going. Knowing Nicolas, it's most certainly a top class occasion, went to by the exquisite and rich and where I'll rub hands with them. I'm clearly going to choke out seeing them swagger around haughtily and effortless, discussing their way of life and having a ball like crazy.

Golly. I inhaled out, assuage the ride was finished lastly, I get to meet Nicolas and energetically reprimand him on why he pulled this amazement on me. The nervousness returned with full power as I examined where we are. My heart skirted a thump, this building is so recognizable, exactly the same structure my previous organization is facilitating their celebration and yes exactly the same I was offered the distinction to sort out. I've completely neglected today is the d day for the occasion.

"Later dear, I leave you here try to clean it up and then the boss entered, seeing you right now I won't question that." Her voice drew me from my stare. She winked at me, waving as the vehicle dashed away.

There were bunches of paparazzi around and honorary pathway where big names stood, giving phony grins and allowing meetings to the press and furthermore taking pictures.

I take out my telephone to call Nicolas, he can't simply request that his kin give me this entire makeover, bring me here and afterward leave me abandoned. Hello it's Nicolas, sympathetically leave a message I'm somewhat occupied, much appreciated. Once more, I attempted and it was till something similar.

Gosh so what I'm I going to do now. I can't go inside passing myself as a representative of the Santiago organization when I've stopped and I even don't want to focus on that dare brained fallen angel. I would prefer to gorge on tequila, margarita and martini which I disdain and never tasted before than that. All things considered I've never tasted liquor so I don't have the foggiest idea how it's like.

I dismissed, prepared to stroll to a less jam-packed spot to sit tight for Nicolas and call him and make him mindful I've shown up so he comes shot in the arm. A shadow and a tap on my shoulders made me anxious, I pivoted in dismay just to see a grinning man who isn't Nicolas before me. He wasn't Nicolas definitely and wasn't monstrous by the same token. He was the inverse, he resembles a dag nab model for play kid with his awful kid look, constructed body, those dimples and white even teeth. "Can I call you Miss Valentina Romeo?"

"Yes, please." He chuckled at my response and then shook my hand.

"Good to meet you, my name is Alejandro." Giving me a hot grin as he found me, also licking his lips.

"OK." I briefly answered, currently exhausted with this convo, presentation or whatever since he chose to eye me like meat and lick his lips. Sorry boo, that' doesn't work with me. I internally feigned exacerbation.

"Accompany me excellent, I've been shipped off escort you." Can't Nicolas come for me himself, or is this piece of all his entire amazement? I followed him nothing less. The paparazzi flung at us, seeing us. Nah scratch that more like seeing Alejandro with me, I'm no VIP for they to be keen on me.

One of them pushed his mouthpiece before him, "Alejandro, who's this adjacent to you? We saw you some time before you enter with America Donato, your sweetheart."

"Is it safe to say that you are two over?"

"Might it be said that she is your side chick?"

"Are you playing them both." They continued to toss inquiries at him. He gave them an exhausted look, driving a camera away from his face and kept quiet. He wouldn't concede them a meeting for them to get the most recent features for their tattle magazines tomorrow first thing as he held my hand and strolled us from them.

I was unable to be more happy. Their brilliant lights and blazing cameras were blinding my eyes as of now. I think I'll require glasses to stroll around thereafter, famous people are doing great adapting to every one of these. I don't know to most recent a moment if I were in their shoes.

We came to inside the structure. The function was going all out, men resembling Greek divine beings who've quite recently slid from Mount Olympus in extravagant tuxedos stood bantering relaxed with rich, tasteful ladies who were holding unto their arms, respecting them and devouring them like bits of meat.

He accompanied me to a table and pardoned himself saying he planned to call my date not before he winked at me. I feigned exacerbation so that him might see which he did and grinned without a consideration.

"Who are you?" An unclear voice whispered to me from the other side of the table. I hadn't really recognized different tenants of the table so I didn't have the foggiest idea what their identity was. This one was a blondie, wearing an in-vogue party dress and her nose lingered palpably as though this spot smelled of cow waste.

"I can tell you for free she has no wealth associated with her name, they're the same either way. They need conducts." Someone else said in contempt. She was a blondie as well and resembled the first. On more intensive look, I got to realize they were twins, their similarity is evidence enough and furthermore the manner in which their noses lingered palpably. Run of the mill rich egotists.

I was going to open my mouth, basically to murmur a statement of regret however somebody beat me to the punch. "As you truly do have precious stones to your name, your couple of dollars doesn't making you rich, discussing most extravagant." She said, positioning her foreheads to challenge them to come at her with a rebound.

"Tsk." And the table was quiet. I covertly recognized the woman close to me. She shut them up with few words which weren't mean.

"Many thanks."

"Nah don't make reference to. I can't stand these Joaquin twins, they choke out me with simply their appearance." Huh? The Joaquin twins? The twins who notwithstanding the wealth of their folks have decided to star just in express and x appraised films are sitting directly before me and I didn't remember them. How might I when they look a lot prettier face to face. Sadly, their attractiveness is a waste on the grounds that their mentality smells, similar to crap. "Hi I like your necklace, is it made specifically for you? Where did you get it from cause I genuinely need a piece of that!"

The woman whose name I don't have any idea yet looks recognizable and saved me from the twins shouted making the others on the table direct their concentration toward us, "Uh actually...." from griddle to fire. I've been saved from those rich twins to being tested by one more affluent woman over a gems, I have no clue how much cash it costs.

"Cayetano, will you let unfortunate young lady be?"

Rather than being glad to have been protected from shaming myself before her, I quickly worried hearing that voice. It was so recognizable, it has so often woofed orders at me and the last I heard it, it finished in tears.

"Valentina..."

"YOU!" He's the last individual I need to see at the present time. I so gravely believe that Nicolas should jump out of any place he is and whisk me away from this egotistical fiend.

"Carlos do both of you know one another?" Cayetano Santiago, I presently recall her from those tattle magazines and her unscripted TV drama, Place of Santiago, in which she for the most part includes her family, asked Carlos who just stood, gazing at me.

"Indeed, she's my date."

"What?" I shouted in shock. I wasn't the one to focus on, the twins went along with me in saying it. The others at the table took a gander at him then at me and started murmuring to themselves. I drafted them out, concentrating on this attractive fiend before me. Did I hear him say I'm his date? Nah there's need to be an error here, he clearly can't, can't and cannnoot be.

"I should say this brother, you got a shocking date here. I generally realized you had great desire for ladies however tonights is an exemption."

"I'm lucky to have her, you know how deities have been scarce these last century." He answered me with a smile, actually looking at me with the utmost concentration. The resentment rising within me wasn't to the point of making me wriggle under his look. It just fuelled it up, how might he venture to remain here and express those things like we're awesome of companions. Like he never affronted me days prior? "Sorry women, I must whisk my date away. See you Cayetano."

"Not all that smooth, give me your number and how about we go out at some point." I dialed my number on her telephone, giving it back to her. I can't cracking accept, Cayetano Santiago, business investor and socialite just requested my number and to spend time with me? Oh rapture I feel significant at the present time! Squeeze me, squeeze me.

My bliss was brief. Satan himself pulled at my arms, motioning to me with his eyes to follow him. He slide his hands around my midsection. Notwithstanding the ladies around the table who were fainting with desire and I would have rather not caused a ruckus and a moron of myself, I would have yanked it away from him and let him know my psyche.

I gave a phony grin to a couple who halted us, creeping nearer to him in spite of myself to give make a pleasant impression. The woman was more inspired by Carlos than the man close to her. Her eyes joyfully devouring his body exotically and the manner in which her hands so seriously needed to grasp him and remove his garments. Are rich ladies this horny 100% of the time?

"Who's this magnificence Lui? The freshest expansion to your assortment?" The man inquires with a conceited smile as he also found me and down, eyes full with craving. He was asking like I wasn't there and I was a piece of object to be gathered.

"Hello sir, I'm not the most beautiful in his list of variety, I'm a human with blood in running through my vein and I have feelings not some toys he can simply throw around would it be advisable for him he get exhausted!" I really wanted to lash out at the one who frowned at me, muttering things softly. It obviously shows he's not used to individuals facing him. Well really awful, I just did it and I'll rehash it would it be advisable for him he affront me with his words.

I heard Carlos laugh alongside me, making me annoyed the more. He's the explanation this man is rambling and there's nothing left but to laugh. I will get you. "I'll see both of you around definitely?" We left immediately he told them to that.

"True Carlos." The woman's sexy voice shared with him as she fluttered her long phony hits at him. He just heaved and glowered at her.

At the point when we were out of general visibility, I moved in an opposite direction from him, making his hand on my midriff fall limp to his side. I turned indignantly towards him, standing akimbo. "Don't even think about contacting me or approach me. How might you venture to bring me here underhandedly, I can go to the police and educate them or far more atrocious those paparazzi out there. I'm certain they're truly passing on for a delicious story at this moment."

"Listen Valentina, I had no way out. I was using up all available time and I had no date. You were the only one I could count, it could never have been correct in the event that I came alone, my vocation and notoriety."

"Ha, it never puzzles me since everything is generally about you! You, you, you, Carlos just you! Never thinking often about those sensations of others insofar as you're cheerful eventually. God realizes how I'm keeping up with my cool and being here with you at this moment."

He pulled at his hair, moaning in disappointment, "I know, I know. This is difficult, it's troublesome in any event, for me however I simply need to say I'm..." He was unable to close his sentence. He was there gazing at me and looking somewhere else, contending energetically to get the words out. It doesn't matter at all to me anything he needs to say. All I need right currently is leave, far away from him and this climate I can never have a place him.

Like he told me, they're no different either way, pompous rich people. "You what?"

"I'm...."

"Gracious so you're puzzled at this point. This is an incredible sight, the incomparable Carlos Santiago is without precedent for his life shy of words and before who? A woman underneath his group. Hey now people well that is news!" I'm amazed at my own unexpected certainty and being capable say this, without feeling no regret except for just displeasure.

"Damn it Valentina I'm..." Indeed, he halted there and never proceeded.

"Gracious Carlos, don't punish me by not talking, scream out because I know what you are capable of. Indeed, even on that day you weren't at speechlessness like this, you gladly alluded to me as a skank! What other brutal and mean words haven't you said before that you're not ready to speak." I recognized hurt streak clearly as I said the word prostitute. He immediately turned away, breathing truly hard. "You know something, your presence is choking out me and getting me got dried out so look for me when you get comfortable with yourself."

What's more, with those final words, I sashayed away and flipped my hair, leaving a confused Carlos to himself.

Chapter Seventeen

Carlos's POV

Where could that imbecile be?

For what reason is Alejandro keeping long in investigating her? Could it be said that he is attempting his tease conversation starters on her? Or on the other hand stand by, Valentina didn't come. In any case, I instructed them also my name, inept specialists! They can't make a solitary showing. I will not acknowledge she didn't come, I'll be ill-fated, she's my last expectation this evening, the only one I could imagine to save me like she has been doing. I trust my best representative not to flop however at that point again she quit, that wouldn't shock me at all on the off chance that she didn't make it.

I tap my left feet restlessly on the floor as I trusted that Alejandro will illuminate me assuming he has seen Valentina and has accompanied her inside the setting. I saw that dare brained dearest companion of mine oncoming with a young lady who's not his sweetheart adjacent to him with his hands around her midriff. I don't get why he actually plays around with individuals while he's having a sweetheart. Why get a name when there are bounty fishes in the ocean, you can look over and not stall out with one. That's the reason I don't do connections. "Can it be guessed that she is here?"

"Yah man she's at the socialite table, you terrible you know, you never let me know your associate is this lovely. She's one fine piece of craftsmanship, the smooth executioner bends and that-"

"Many thanks to you Alejandro, I will go get her." I cut him off rudely. I'm out of nowhere irate hearing him portray Valentina subsequent to getting to look at her excellence and body when I've not had the option to do as such. I ought to have been the main individual to see her tragically I was an over-the-top pussy.

I left them to go on with what they were doing for sure they need to do. After much trouble of dodging parched young ladies, I observe my direction to the table he said Valentina is at.

I tracked down her sitting close to Cayetano, my oldest sister. Cayetano was grinding away again as she pointed with fantastic eyes to the choker on Valentina's neck. I know without hearing what she's asking, she adores the adornments and would need one. Normal her, continuously gathering style things just to look the best out there and in her unscripted TV drama.

"Cayetano will you let the poor young lady be?" I needed to save Valentina seeing her at speechlessness as she shot her eyes around, looking for a remark.

"Valentina...." all what I needed to say was left in my mouth as I gazed at her the second she pivoted. My goodness my, a heavenly messenger recently slid.

Valentina is looking past lovely this evening, the make up sat idle, she was fairly increasing the value of the make up and that white shining dress, gosh it has completely fitted her and drawn out those bends of hers making her resemble a holy messenger. No big surprise Alejandro was fainting over her. I'm the most fortunate to have her as my date this evening. So entrancing.

"YOU!" She shrieked at me, noticeably irate.

"Lui do both of you know one another?" Cayetano asked checking out at me and afterward at her.

"Indeed, she's my date."

"What? "The Joaquin twins and Valentina said in unison. The vibe of doubt composed all around her face and afterward she looked disheartened like she was expecting another person.

"If I must confess bro, you had an amazing date here. I generally realized you had great desire for ladies yet tonight's is an exemption."

"I'm privileged to have her, you know how scarce divinities have been in the last century." I agree with Cayetano, Valentina is like a spirit, the most excellent lady on earth on this planet. Abruptly, I began feeling regret for the horrendous things I shared with her. I really want to move her away from here and set things straight, I want to tell her how sorry I am and that I won't ever do that to her from this point forward.

After that I'll convince her to return to the workplace, her work area and my life. I want her around there more than she knows, these days without her have been horrendous, I've turned around into mean grouchy boss.

I remained here trusting that Cayetano will take her number. I'm happy she prefers her, really she's the only one in our family who couldn't care less about somebody's experience prior to being companions or loving them. Most of us are uhm well, erm what you definitely know.

I really wanted to slide my hand around her minuscule midriff which fitted completely in my grasp, similar to it was made for it. She's warm and smelling superb. Could I at any point get an embrace please, I need just have her in my arms and breathe in her aroma, Valentina doesn't need that, she's strained and seems as though she needs to be not even close to me. That damages yet I merit it.

"Who is this magnificence Lui?" The freshest expansion to your assortment?" My uncle, Bautista Santiago asked me, peering toward her up. He had a more youthful woman next to him, yet wasn't keen on checking out at her than my Valentina. I need to punch his face, sadly he's family and family before hoes.

"Hello sir, I'm not is kind compare to the beautiful ones out there. I'm a human with sentiments and feelings not some article or toy he can throw around would it be advisable for him to get exhausted." Ah so she's this cheeky? Valentina furiously spoke harshly to Uncle Bautista who gritted his teeth, contradicting her. Men in my family prefer not to be gone against and here is one.

"I'll see you all around definitely?" I want to move us away from them before Uncle Bautista explodes. His mouth had zero channel and his heart has no mankind. He will corrupt Valentina so low; she won't wish she was ever conceived. I can't remain here and witness all that.

"Sure Carlos." His whore, told me. He has a spouse and youngsters yet indecently circumvents laying down with young ladies mature enough to be his nieces. I don't get why he does that, Aunt Caramel is a genuine stunner, a previous belle of the ball, maybe she's revolting. In the event that I at any point get hitched which I exceptionally question, I'm never going to betray my wife.

I strolled ahead not caring a whole lot to that whore and focused more on the thing I will say now that I am separated from everyone else with her. "Don't even think about contacting me or approach me. How might you venture to bring me here underhandedly I can go to the police and inform them or surprisingly more dreadful those paparazzi out there. I'm certain they're truly kicking the bucket for a delicious story at the present time." She moved in an opposite direction from me, telling at me the second we were out from public eye.

"Listen Valentina, I had no way out. I was using up all available time and I had no date. You were the only one I could count, it could not have possibly been correct on the off chance that I came alone, my vocation and notoriety." How might I say this for her to know how sorry I am.

"Ha, it never astounds me since everything is generally about you! You, you, you, Carlos just you! Never thinking often about those sensations of others insofar as you're cheerful eventually. God realizes how I'm keeping up with my cool and being with you at the present time."

I pulled at my hair, moaning in dissatisfaction, "I know, I know. This is difficult, it's troublesome in any event, for me however I simply need to say I'm..." The s word wouldn't leave my mouth. It's something I don't recollect telling anyone in long stretches of my reality.

"You what?"

"I'm...." Please accept my apologies! That is the very thing I need to say. Valentina I'm heartbroken. I'm being a simpleton expressing it in my mind and not from my lips. I wish I had my something that I can compose on and give it to her.

"Goodness so you're dumbfounded at this point. This is an amazing sight, the incomparable Carlos Santiago is without precedent for his life short for words and before who? A woman beneath his group. Hey now people well that is news!"

"Damn it Valentina I'm..." Why for heaven's sake wont this word leave my lips!

"Goodness Lui, don't humiliate me by hushing up, shout out with a full power like the man you are on the grounds that I realize what you're able to do.

Indeed, even on that day you weren't at speechlessness like this, you gladly alluded to me as a whore! What other brutal and mean words haven't you said before that you're not ready to speak. You know something, your presence is choking out me and getting me dried out so look for me when you get comfortable with yourself."

I was left harmed and furious. I was unable to say the damn word and Valentina didn't improve the situation with her cheeky mentality. She flipped her hair at me and sashayed away. I should concede that was so damn attractive and the manner in which her butt was wiggling too with each progression. Damn! I need a piece of that fine ass.

Isabella's POV

Damn Isabella that was cheeky. I commended myself for having the option to unhesitatingly say those words to Carlos. I cherished how he was puzzled and attempted to spread the news yet proved unable, the expression all over is something I need to drink a glass of champagne to, to commend my triumph over him.

I made a beeline for the food segment of the dance hall, especially to the bar and sat down on a stool. The server pushed a glass of a fluid I have no clue I'm front of me. Is it safe to say that he is wired giving me a beverage I've not arranged? Or on the other hand is this piece of the celebration? I don't recollect including that. "What's this?"

"Pètrus wine." He responded and continued attending to the others.

"I didn't ask this." I called his attention and told him to take it back, because there is no way I'm going to drink this, think of a situation in which it's spiked. To get me tranquilized and perhaps assault me or something like that?

"Of a truth I know, he did." He said with a fatigued look, beckoning to someone close to me. I changed my look to the individual alongside me, a man with spiky Valeria hair and with the kid nearby look. He had this haughty grin all over, I needed to clear off.

"Hello attractive." He slurred his words, liquor radiating from his mouth. Ewww, nauseating. I simply disdain the smell of liquor and this person here is toasted the center when the closeout hasn't begun.

"Cut the tease, I didn't request that you get me a beverage."

"I prefer my girls sneaky and squandered; they scream the sexiest."

"I'm not and won't ever be your young lady." I said with aversion. Who does he even think he is, requesting for me a beverage just to get to lay down with me. Holy cow! Did I come to experience in this world because of debased men?

"Hello simple child, I'm going to." He came towards me and held my midsection firmly and endeavored to crush his lips on mine. I sidestepped the kiss and battled in his hold as I pushed him off me with my mind which weren't really amazing. He fixed his grasp and before I knew, he lurched back, gripping his side and murmuring in torment.

"Get your disgusting hands off her Camilo!" A voice I know too very much shouted indignantly at the my assaulter. I was happy, somebody has acted the hero regardless of whether it's him.

Carlos unclenched his fingers and came towards me. He measured my cheeks, scanning my face for injuries or imprints and my body as well, "would you say you are OK Valentina? Did he hurt you?"

Obviously, I'm not OK. Who will be in the wake of being attacked? "No doubt I'm fine, Uh I'm alright." I told him and eliminated his hands that were all the while measuring my cheeks. I loved the way they were warm and some kind of solace to me however nah, he's Carlos, he can never be a blanket to anyone. I don't have the foggiest idea about his expectations for saving me.

"Great since, supposing that you're not, he's a dead man." He then, at that point, went to Camilo, "assuming I at any point see you even close to her once more, view yourself as a carcass."

The person wouldn't hear any of it. He progressed nearer to Carlos and grasped his hand into a clench hand, swinging it towards him, no me in light of the fact that in my endeavor to drive Carlos away, I got the clench hand. Presently my nose is harming so awful, I feel like it's falling, a particularly absurd choice on my part. "Huh what are you going to do? Kill me? I don't fear you Carlos."

Seeing what he had done, Carlos charged towards him like a furious bull and punched him in all spots imaginable with Camilo fighting back weakly. At this point a group had begun to shape, fortunately nobody had taken out their telephone to tape the entire thing. It will be a complete catastrophe would it be advisable for them they have; I can picture the features early tomorrow first thing.

I remained there not knowing what to do, I'm the explanation these two men are battling and fighting like monsters. If by some stroke of good luck I had paid attention to what Carlos needed to say and not come here, I could never have gotten this horrendous nose and he wouldn't battle at the present time. It's all my issue! "Carlos if it's not too much trouble, stop, would you like to kill him?"

He either didn't hear my yells for him to stop or he simply needed to fulfill his fighting craving. He continued to toss punches at him, the man was currently feeble and couldn't avoid yet had the mouth to holler at Carlos to punch harder in light of the fact that he was unable to feel anything. I can't watch this nitwit kick the bucket, no. I'll be faulted for this and Carlos will be justified, he has the cash.

I need to give My best. I went towards Carlos and orbited my hands around his midsection, to pull him off him. He strained at my touch and stop mid air in giving another punch. Incredible, I prevailed with regards to inspiring him to stop. I removed his hand and hauled him from the scene, he followed dutifully and not once did he fight. It was like he was hypnotized by my touch.

Chapter Eighteen

Isabella's POV

"Uh Mr. Santiago.." I said weakly, tinkering with my fingers. He turned his head towards me at his name being referenced and taken a gander at me eagerly, "I need to say thank you for saving me back there." I wouldn't realize what might have occurred in the event that he hadn't shown up there on schedule to save me from that man which didn't end well yet for he saving me, I'm appreciative and believe him should be aware.

"Don't bother." He just said and traded his deliberation back to the host, who was broadcasting the morals for the quiet closeout. Carlos and I are presently at an alternate table at the back, it was simply us and there is quiet between us since we arrived. I had a liquor sanitizer in my grip which I utilized with my cloth to take care of his ridiculous knuckles. Not once did he wince to show how excruciating it was, it's like he's made of steel and there again I'm not astonished, an inhumane man like is most certainly made of steel.

He is outrageously tranquil as am I. I disdain this quietness here, I maintain that him should break it, let me know what he needed to share with me or simply anything you know to cut this thick quietness.

He made no endeavor to express anything as he stayed there, confronting different visitors and pulling at his hair now and again. I've known him for a brief time frame to realize he's baffled. I want to give his hand or thigh a delicate press, to comfort him however nah, he's most certainly going to get pissed and will have a more motivation to affront me, nah I'm great.

My ringtone fell off, demonstrating I had a call. I took out my telephone and saw it was Nicolas calling, I got it right away, "hello Nicolas... you know it's cute..yeah no doubt, it was a misconception that has proactively been taken consideration off.. obviously I'll see you at work tomorrow..yeah bye, goodnight dear."

I got Lui check me out. His face was in a glower and his eyes were perilously dull. What? What have I expressed wrong here to merit that look. I feigned exacerbation and turn away. He's being a numbskull, overlooking me and afterward lashing out when another person chose to converse with me. Truly what's his concern? He ought to offer me a reprieve. Tsk, tsk.

My displeasure evaporated and my consideration was totally taken by one doll face, Cayetano's teacup Maltese which I've seen so often in her show, magazines and news is available to be purchased, looking a la mode like its proprietor, in her pink sparkle coat and matching headband.

I'm absolutely enamored with the canine and I want to get it however nah, I don't have that sort of the means to purchase her. There's nothing left but to gaze at her groggily as I'm doing now and let the rich women around get it. A considerable lot of them were fainting over the canine and promptly tapped on their gadget, putting their offers. May the most extravagant success. I moaned and proceeded with my gaze. For what reason might I at any point be abruptly rich and purchase this doll, see it's smooth fur and little dog face, mwah mwah.

The little dog invested in some opportunity to get off the deals table and soon the closeout was finished, she was the last thing to be sold. I hurled out, eased. I can at last leave and return home to my bed which is by all accounts calling out for me. I'm coming child.

"Valentina." Carlos shouted to me, referencing my name like it was the most valuable word of all time.

I adored how it sounded when he said it now, charming. "Allow me to get you home."

I would not get up from my seat. That sentence was supposed to be at some point prior and it didn't end well. No chance I'm I leaving here with him, I'd prefer walk as far as possible home than do that. I nodded my head, "I appreciate, I'm fine."

"Try not to be obstinate, I won't leave you halfway. I vow to send you home this time around." Goodness so he recalls what he did and he acted the greatest day as though, he sat idle. Tsk, I saw his face to check whether he was playing a prank on me. He looked earnest and was grinning as well.

I said nothing and got up from my seat, taking grip from my table. He composed on his telephone, securing it prior to placing it in his pocket, "we should go." He drove the way as we battled for strolling space among the thick group and were nearly at the entryway and out of the setting without taking someone into account calling out to me.

It was Mr. Santiago the senior. He danced towards us with a demeanor of certainty, grinning and wishing individuals goodnight. "Ok Valentina dear, you're looking superb this evening."

"Much obliged to you sir."

"Alright, I will need to be at the office tomorrow, there are things we need to trash and it's urgent. I won't burn through your time so you can get a decent rest and come early. Goodnight." He didn't give me the chance to let him know I've stopped. He left just subsequent to saying goodnight and I remained there not knowing whether I ought to follow him and make him mindful or simply go.

Anxious Carlos made a sound as if to speak and tapped his foot, a sign he's in a rush. I feigned exacerbation and followed him the whole way to his limo, the one I utilized in coming here.

Interestingly, he looked out for me. I was left stunned, who is this man and how has he treated Carlos?

He sat close to me and requested his escort to drive the vehicle. We were together and alone, quiet encompassing us as I turn away from him and disapproving of my business. I felt his look drill openings on me, going to take a gander at him, I swallowed.

His eyes had obscured as they meandered my body erotically. I felt uncovered under his look and unexpectedly the air is hot, incredibly hot. I became terrified, imagine a scenario where he pulls that trick on me once more. Where will I go? I can't simply fly through of the window.

I hurried somewhat away from him which I didn't go unrecognized by him.

He hurried closer to me making me return until my back hit the window, simply extraordinary now I'm caught. He grinned, "run everything you can yet you can't stow away," and circumnavigated my midriff with his hands, pulling me nearer to him to the degree we were contacting skin to skin, our garments being the main obstruction.

He curved my head and carried his lips to my neck, delicately sucking on it and following it up to my ear, that touchy part. Causing me to solidify and attempt to pull him away from him. He was so solid, my weak hands couldn't pull him off me, right when he made an endeavor to lick it, the vehicle ground to a halt. I'm home, thank you sky.

I was marginally frustrated on the grounds that I needed to feel how it will be like, I've perused such countless sentiment books and I realize their moves yet I've never attempted them, this evening was my opportunity and it exploded into smoke in light of the escort. Would it be a good idea for me I say thanks to him or admonish him?

Carlos murmured fuck faintly and crawled away from me, not prior to murmuring hazardously into my ears, "I'll see you at the workplace tomorrow Dee perhaps we can go on from where we've stopped."

Truly, Dee? Is that the name he could think of? I made a sound as if to speak in shame and moving awkwardly, his hands were still around my abdomen and banishing me from escaping the vehicle. "Mr. Santiago, your hands."

"Nobody knows the amount I disdain getting them off her midsection and allowing her to get into her home." He murmured to himself however I heard it. I become flushed regardless of myself, I was as yet irate at him for what he did and presently. It's like he was exploiting we being separated from everyone else to rehash that and idiotic me needed to encounter it this time around.

Carlos delivered me, escaping the vehicle and looking out for me. He then strolled me to our entryway and gazed at my face, my body and my face again prior to wishing me goodnight, this while his eyes, obscuring. I smell desire in the air, and tragically I need it too.

What is getting into you Isabella? Simply this evening and a little private time with him has gotten me all worked up? I become flushed and immediately made for the entryway, making my butt wiggle. Such thing will not go unrecognized by that sick person behind me, I heard him mutter, damn that ass. Men will constantly be men regardless of how rich, poor, attractive or appalling they are.

Chapter Nineteen

Isabella's POV

Once more, my morning timer sounded, I wasn't snoozing this time around for it to be an aggravation. I didn't really rest, what unfolded in the vehicle was at the forefront of my thoughts the entire evening.

What was it that he needs to accomplish by doing that? Demonstrate to himself, I have some sort of affections for him yet the examine his eyes were in opposition to that. Maybe he had some kind of affections for me.

Perhaps I'm perusing to much significance into this entire thing. I bet he's not pondering it this moment, to him I'm simply one more young lady he needs on his bed. Please accept my apologies to dishearten him since, I'm not and I won't ever be one of those young ladies. I was so silly engaging his idiotic activities yesternight, I ought to have smacked him across the face to send the message to him.

I looked heavenwards, expressing a quiet petition and asking absolution from God for practically surrendering to desire.

I then, at that point, jumped up and advanced toward the washroom to clean up and prepare to meet Mr. Santiago the boss. Didn't his child educate him regarding me stopping and the conditions encompassing it? Or on the other hand was he such a large amount a weakling to do that?

There were hints of cosmetics all over and the enlarged nose I got yesterday, which made me take a more drawn out time than expected in the bathroom. I got once again into my room and took the work garments, I had prepared to wear for work at Chapman Hardware today and put on all the cosmetics abilities I know in concealing the injury on my nose.

I want to settle on a decision to Nicolas and clear up the circumstance for him. It will be terrible of me not to and I realize very well the way that disheartened he will be assuming I tell him. I must choose between limited options than to meet my previous chief, he's an old man who has gotten my appreciation such a long time I've worked under him and today, I need to show him that equivalent regard.

I'm presently all set and as I search for my siphons, I run over the sack in which the dress and adornments from yesterday are in. I'll wash the dress today when I get back and hand it over to him tomorrow. I can't keep it and I will not it is possible that, he will believe I'm taking care of his cash. When does he never believe that?

Carlos's POV

Seeing Camilo badgering Valentina made my head spin with rage to the most elevated point. I just saw red the moment I arrived and saw him firmly grasping her midsection and attempting to kiss her. Poor people young lady was battling and that weakling in his squandered state was too heedless to even think about seeing.

"Get your foul hands off her Camilo. "I punched his ribs so hard which sent him faltering and moving away from Valentina. Next time he needs to meddle with somebody, it certainly ought not be my Isabella, sorry Valentina.

"Can it be assumed that you are fine Valentina? Did he hurt you?" I asked her, measuring her cheeks and meandering my eyes all over assuming that bastard challenge hurt her.

"Definitely I'm fine, Uh I'm OK."

"Nice since, assuming that you're not fine, he's a goner," "if I at any time see you close to her again, consider yourself a dead man." I screamed at that weakling. I couldn't care less; I'll simply kill him and arrange off his body flawlessly without a follow Whatsoever. I have companions in the mafia you know.

Appears as though a few weaklings have out of nowhere gotten all striking and solid, since they've gazed working out and acquiring biceps. He got up and came towards me, pointing his child clench hand at me. I felt no feeble knuckles all over, I heard a whine from Valentina. "Huh what are you going to do? Kill me? I don't fear you, Carlos."

Somebody's a dead body at the present time. Say your last supplication moron. He just swung his clench hand at my Dee? Ha, I charged towards him like the monster I am the point at which I'm angered and punched him in all spots imaginable where it will hurt like a bitch.

That bastard like the quitter he is, couldn't hit me back yet just hollered at me to beat him more. I know it's his method for outlining himself as the person in question yet I couldn't care less. Nobody raises a finger at any adored one of mine and goes scot free.

"Carlos kindly stop, would you like to kill him?" I decided to disregard her yells, me punching him isn't about Valentina alone, it's about Cayetano as well. This imbecile here attempted to assault her and later outlined her for it.

I was unable to manage him then in light of my folks and my administration. I'm not letting this chance of showing this weakling something new never to screw with a Santiago cruise me by.

How does that vibe like bitch? I gazed at his blood-splashed face. He's a forlorn wreck at this moment however it couldn't be so awful giving him a last punch, will it? Simply a last to exercise authority over him is around here since he isn't apprehensive about me.

My last punch wasn't given, Valentina's hands circumnavigated my midriff and I hardened at her touch. It resembled a can of super cold water, gradually however successfully extinguishing this seething fire I am.

I got off him and quietly followed Valentina to any place she was sending me.

She carried me to the lobby where the bartering was going to begin and kept an eye on my horrendous knuckles with a sanitizer. The one I found her utilizing to wipe her table the day I gave her Sofia's red strap to arrange off.

Everything through she doing that, I stayed silent, my brain meandered as I second guessed myself why I lashed out seeing Camilo with her. Could I have gone to thump him in the event that it was another young lady? Or then again was this on the grounds that she helped me to remember Isabella?

I don't have the foggiest idea, I don't, perhaps it was my humankind that took the best of me that second. I want to believe that she's excused me for those terrible words I told her in my room.

I needed to scrutinize her in the event that I've made up for myself in her eyes and apologize in the event that I haven't. She didn't allow me the opportunity to do so then, at that point.

I was unable to force myself to say the s word even after she said thanks to me for saving her life. I was battling inside me to exclaim it and put it behind me yet nah, it didn't come out.

It's ideal on the off chance that I just stayed silent and not embarrass myself before her as I did previously. I wouldn't see any problems her sashaying endlessly once more and wiggling her butt again so that me could see.

I stayed there, fantasizing about her butt. Figuring how it will feel like in my grasp as I massage them like batter. My dreams were sliced short as I paid attention to her discussion to whoever was on the telephone with her. She was looking blissful and grinning, conversing with the individual and I heard her call him dear.

Young ladies possibly grin while they're conversing with their beaus or crush. It's a reality, they rather frown and affront their closest companions or sisters. Who's this extraordinary individual in her life who makes her grin as she did next to me. I don't recall getting that somewhat grin from her and it completely made me mad.

Also, she referenced work tomorrow. Has she found a new line of work currently in the wake of stopping with a simple secretarial testament that isn't so amazing it is outdated to think about that sort of declaration? I will not permit her go work anyplace. She's in an ideal situation working under me. Me, just I ought to be her chief and not another person. I know exactly what to do. I sent a speedy message to father letting him know Valentina was searching for him.

I know how the elderly person loves her for her effectiveness and he came sooner than anticipated, meeting at the door. I laughed inside me perceiving how befuddled she was after Father advised her to meet him at work tomorrow.

So it's true, she's currently my worker. I can get to see a greater amount of her lovely face and attractive body the entire day.

Discussing her body, every one of the frightful contemplations I had about her and dreams returned into memory as she and I are separated from everyone else in my limo.

How might that ass feel like? Furthermore, I gravely need to lick that spot behind her ear, the one they say is touchy and those delectable stout lips. Envision Granny twerking for Granddad. Well, that is hilarious.

I envisioned only anything to get these contemplations off of my mind. I don't believe that her should feel and think like I'm pulling the second piece of what I did in my room on her.

Eleven Hours Later

I'm pulling at my hair in dissatisfaction. I can't stand the fact that Valentina an I will be in the same car, how her neckline was so extraordinarily sweetened as I sucked on it and her vanilla perfume. "Gosh!"

She will be here any moment from now and this ain't making a difference. I can't take a gander at her considering these contemplations and I have zero faith in myself not to rehash indeed how I treated her yesternight.

"Sir, there's a woman here to see you. She says she's Valentina Romeo, your own aide." Amalia informed me on the telephone.

"Let her come in." How is it best I respond? Dislike I haven't seen her previously. In any case, with these contemplations, it's ideal on the off chance that I occupied myself with something so I don't see her face or body by the same token.

Who I'm I joking? Valentina entered my office. I knew it just by her vanilla fragrance which immediately occupied the room.

I took a look at her, she was looking adorable in her white and Valeria body con dress with matching yield coat, extremely unobtrusive.

I busied myself perusing the organization's pamphlet and possibly looked into when she welcomed me, "Great morning Valentina, how's your   nose?"

"It's fine as you can see." It was to be sure fine yet it

was looking excessively light contrasted with her skin tone.

"As times goes on, don't be satisfactorily irrational to get in the center of a fight." She might have been more injured than she is now all for the love of whiskey.

"I've taken in my example." She said and gave me an envelope.

"What's this? "I battered it in my grip, containing money's unduly light.

"My resignation letter. "Her face was indifferent, no discontentment or smile.

Well that is a stunner, why? Didn't father persuade her to remain? Isn't it what he is great at? Nah, nah I can't neglect her from me a subsequent time. Her nonappearance in this office has cost me an incredible arrangement, call me self-centered or any name however I can't release her. "Plunk down Miss Romeo." It's no time like the present I utilized my definitive voice on her. "Also, what are your reasons?"

"I don't figure you ought to ask that, you and I realize already. "She said in a virus tone and took a gander at me dangerous.

"Have you told my dad?"

"Isn't his office what I'm accustomed to?"

"Then, as it is now, do you think he knows you're leaving and has agreed to it, you can't go. I'm the manager around here and he isn't, I take every one of the choices concerning the organization and not him. So, Miss Romeo, I request you to return to your office. This conversation is finished, I'm now exhausted." I yawned to add more distortion to it.

Valentina stayed there not knowing what to say and glaring blades at me. In the event that looks could kill, I'll be in a body pack at this moment. "Do I have to rehash the same thing to you?"

"Maybe you need to revise it yourself so you know the amount of an ass you're being, you can't make me to work for you on the probability that I would rather not."

I applauded and sneered, "I can't compel you to work for me since you should work here and think about who's the chief? Me! Your endorsement isn't anything out there, my dad showed compassion for you since you possess intellect and your agreement with my organization says you can stop following five years. Also, how long have you been here? One? Two? No, simply a year and half, who do you hope to finish the other years?"

"Aargh! "She screeched angrily and stood up from her seat advancing towards me. I should say she's looking more hotter irate and with her nose erupting. "Try not to think you've gotten me attached to your organization, recollect Carlos, I'll be out through the entryway and at no point ever return here in the future, you know why? Since the five years is up."

"I realize I know and think about what child? The five years isn't up so you work for me, how does that sound?" I grinned at her, thoroughly partaking in her glance at me with lethal eyes, "return to your work area child young lady, you know I'm not this indulgent." I waved my hand at her contemptuously.

Valentina feigned exacerbation at me and stomped off, her butt was doing that wiggle. Before long I will crush it and perceive how it believes, it's being an allurement as of now.

I present myself with a glass of bourbon and toast to my shrewd self. I've overseen some way or another to inspire her to remain, presently I need to deal with saying 'sorry' as far as she might be concerned, to bring harmony between us cause I'm not cherishing these little battles however I just own it's charming.

Chapter Twenty

Isabella's POV

I want to wipe that egotism and sneer all over and choke him too when I'm finished. That is dolt cornered me as it were, I'll always be unable to win. How idiotic of me to figure I could effectively leave this organization and go somewhere else when my authentication is a wreck: it's obsolete, so out of the framework and I want to get a new one.

If by some stroke of good luck Carlos resembled his dad, I'll be gone and working at the Chapmans. Presently I'm trapped in this hellhole with a butt sphincter for a chief, a man I need just to move away from. How might I get by? You did it before Isabella and you will even presently. Simply don't allow him to get to you. I surmise this is what I got to do.

"Miss Romeo, get into my office." His irritating voice rang via telephone indignantly. Simple Isabella, take full breaths. I left my work area, passing by Amalia's. We both share one thing for all intents and purpose, Satan himself. I feel sorry for her for working under Carlos and to the remainder of the staff, they see us to be fortunate being the partners of a praised entertainer, much to their dismay the amount of an ass he is.

I advanced into his office and met him with his tie free on the table and his shirt unfastened up to his navel. He gazed at me perilously like a hunter to his prey. "Care to make sense of this?"

He waved a piece of paper in my face. I recalled that it to be the authority letter I got from Chapman Gadgets the following day I was extended to an employment opportunity. How could he get it? "Make sense of what?"

"This poo! Valentina this, you challenge go despite my good faith to look for work at another organization? Is your five years up as of now?" He said getting perilously near me, I made a stride back.

"Hello, Mr. Santiago, am I mistaken you to be visually impaired. The date is recent, weeks prior and assuming I ought to advise you that was the point at which I quit."

"That cheeky mouth of yours will cause you problems Miss, as a matter of fact it has gotten you into one the present moment and I'm moving to rebuff you." His lips extended into a sneer I should concede is hot.

All of a sudden, he pulled me to his body and stuck me to his work area, his hand laying on my bum. "You've been a terrible agent Valentina so I need to transfer you to the best way." He told me in a philosophical voice that made me shake in an invigorated manner.

Carlos then, at that point, got my bum, crushing it and moaned. My heart began pulsating quick, desire topping me off and blurring faculties as he licked that delicate spot. "Mr. Santiago."

"The reason you are this bold." He released me stepped back, taking a glimpse at my red face and scoffed. "Go back to your work area, I'll reach out to you when it's necessary."

I was left idiotic, befuddled and furious. What's his concern? For what reason did he need to do that to me? I'm not a doll or a manikin that he can call the shots and control me the manner in which he needs and whenever. "For what reason do you do this and what was that for?" He didn't care about me and got some distance from confronting me, pulling at his hair. "Don't you give me the quiet treatment.

"Leave Valentina simply go, far away from me however not this structure, it's actually working hours."

"I don't have any reason to be here with you in the first place." I hurried out of his office out of anger. Chy saw me plunk down with a pissed face and came towards me inquiring as to why I was in that disposition. "I simply need to be without anyone else please."

I excused her and stayed there moping, the email on the PC I was composing isn't fascinating any longer. If by some stroke of good luck I had somebody to converse with, I have little to no faith in Amalia. I can see Camela yet she's distant in Kuwait, visiting her cousins.

Carlos

I got the glass of bourbon and slugged it down my throat, putting the glass down and topping off it. That is the very thing I've been doing since I requested Valentina out of my office.

I was past distraught when I saw the paper lying heedlessly around her work area when I came to the workplace earlier today. I figured out it was an acknowledgment letter from an organization, for her to be a colleague. For what reason would it be a good idea for her she be for another person, she should be for myself and just me!

That crap ain't occurring. I called her into my office to request a substantial clarification just for her to be a shrewd mouth. Carlos doesn't take cheeky comments from individuals particularly ladies, they should submit to me not be at neck length with me.

I considered ways of crashing into her head who the manager is here. The main thing that came into my brain was to snatch her butt, press it in a way she will get stimulated. Ladies are just agreeable then.

Rather than her getting excited, I did. Never had I contacted a bum that delicate and delicious. Terrible thoughts began getting into my head, I needed to stop myself before I went excessively far and she thought twice about it and perhaps this time around not even the agreement with my dad will make her stay.

She's so difficult, continuously addressing things. I needed to pivot and not face her; I have zero faith in myself. One glance at her and I'll be ill-fated. It wasn't masculine of me to holler at her to leave yet that was my main choice assuming I needed her out of my office. Presently I'm a wreck, I don't have any idea what's going on with me. Things shouldn't have been this way; it shouldn't have gotten to this part.

I should inspire her to pardon me not to convince her to can't stand me. I don't figure I can take a gander at her at any point in the future, nah, nah.

Hope you enjoyed the book? Kindly rate the book and recommend if I should continue with the Series 2

WATCH OUT FOR SERIES TWO